90 Miles to Havana

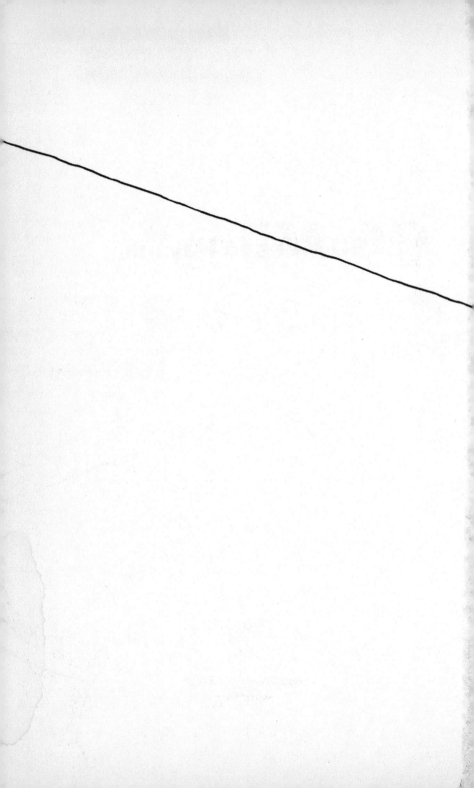

90 Miles to Havana

Enrique Flores-Galbis

Roaring Brook Press
New York

Text copyright © 2010 by Enrique Flores-Galbis
Published by Roaring Brook Press
Roaring Brook Press is a division of Holtzbrinck Publishing
   Holdings Limited Partnership
175 Fifth Avenue, New York, New York 10010
www.roaringbrookpress.com

Distributed in Canada by H. B. Fenn and Company Ltd.

Cataloging-in-Publication Data is on file at the Library of Congress

Roaring Brook Press books are available for special promotions and premiums.
For details contact: Director of Special Markets, Holtzbrinck Publishers.

First Edition August 2010
Book design by Sonia Chaghatzbanian
Printed in June 2010 in the United States of America by RR Donnelley & Sons Company,
Harrisonburg, Virginia

10 9 8 7 6 5 4 3 2 1

To my parents, who were brave enough to let go, and my older brothers
Anibal and Fernando: tormentors, teachers, and titans whom I will
always look up to and love.

90 Miles to Havana

BIG FISH

We're fishing at the edge of the Gulf Stream two miles north of Havana. From this far out, the city looks like it's about to be swallowed by the waves.

"Havana is sinking," I say to Bebo, standing behind the wheel.

"I guess Columbus was right. The earth *is* round," Bebo says without a hint of a smile on his face. He hands me a nautical chart of the north coast of Cuba.

"Check the compass, and the chart—tell me exactly where we are. "

I run my finger across a dark gray band marking the Gulf Stream, then up to the last link in a chain of islands hooking south from the tip of Florida.

"Key West is eighty-five miles north-northeast of us," I say, checking the big brass compass. "Havana is five miles due south. "

"You're getting the hang of it," Bebo says. When my father yawns, Bebo nods toward the stern of the boat. "I think he's had enough for the day."

Papi's been sitting in the fighting chair almost the whole day waiting for a bite, but he hasn't gotten as much as a nibble. He's not too happy about the possibility that we might be going home empty-handed. My father thinks that if we catch a big fish on December 31st we'll have good luck every day of the coming year.

My two brothers and I always go fishing with him on that day. We usually have a few big ones to show my mother and the Garcias, our next-door neighbors, when they meet us at the dock. After the fish are cleaned and put away, we eat dinner and celebrate New Year's Eve on the boat, with the carnival music and revelers playing and dancing in the streets above us.

Papi stretches, then yawns even louder. Bebo whispers, "Hurry, he's going to get up."

I'm standing next to Papi smiling, when he starts to unclip the rod from the chair. The fighting chair is made out of steel and wood, swivels and tilts just like the ones at the barbershop, but it has no cushions. It does have straps and the hardware to clip the rod to the chair so you don't get pulled into the water when you're fighting a big fish.

"Of all the years to go home empty-handed," he says, looking over my head at the horizon.

"Papi, can I take a turn on the chair?" I ask and look around for my brothers. I can hear Gordo and Alquilino, the oldest, buzzing around our next-door neighbor Angelita. They're too busy to notice that Papi has gotten up.

"I'm a lot bigger than I was last year," I add, squaring my shoulders and standing up as straight as I can.

"I don't know, Julian. The fish out here are huge," he says. "A flick of their tail and they'll pull you in!"

"Yeah, but I'm stronger now," I say.

"It's late, Julian. Next time."

"What if there is no next time? I heard you talking to Mr. Garcia on the phone this morning, you said everything is changing and this could be our last fishing trip." Papi is looking at me but I can't tell what he's thinking. "I know what to do, Bebo explained the whole thing to me."

"Bebo explained the whole thing?" he asks as the ends of his mustache start to rise.

"From beginning to end," I say. "And you know how good Bebo is at explaining things."

Papi is sizing me up as if he's never seen me before. "So, do you think you can handle a big fish?"

"I know exactly what to do!" I say with as much confidence as I can muster.

"OK, Julian," he says and squints at the setting sun. "I guess we have time for one more pass."

I jump into the chair as fast as I can, before my brothers can claim it, or Papi can change his mind.

～⋏⋏～

"This is your big chance," my father says and then helps me fit the end of the rod into the metal cup in between my knees. He clips the rod to the brass fittings on the arm of the chair. "There. Now if a big fish wants to pull you in, it'll have to take the chair, too."

I grip the rod tight and set my feet. "I'm ready."

My father smiles at me. "Good. You know the rule, right?"

"Yell, even if it's just a nibble," I say, repeating what he tells everyone that climbs up on the chair.

Papi is staring out at the horizon again but now he's shaking his head. I know he's thinking that it's over for the day—for this year, but you never know. If I catch a big one Papi will get a year's worth of luck, and they'll take a picture of me standing next to the fish hanging upside down on the dock. Out of respect for the fish I'll look real serious to show he put up a good fight.

"Don't worry, Papi. I'll catch one for us," I say to cheer him up.

"That would be nice," he says, and then pats the two cigars in his shirt pocket. He and Bebo always light up on the way home.

Holding the rod firmly in my left hand, I pinch the line between my right thumb and forefinger, just like my father does. The fishing line is slicing into the waves, the green lure spinning beneath the wake, and I can almost see a big silver blue marlin lurking right behind it.

"Julian," Bebo calls. "Don't look at the water. You'll get seasick."

He must have read my mind. "*Sí*, Bebo," I yell and then look up, not at the horizon, but just above it.

Bebo taught me that trick and a thousand others.

He used to drive a truck for my father, but when Papi heard he was a great cook, he convinced him to give up the truck and take up the spoon for our house. Now he cooks, takes care of the boat, and teaches me things. Ever since my brothers stopped letting me hang around with them, Bebo makes sure I have something to do. It doesn't matter what he's doing, he always lets me help.

If he's cooking a paella, he'll show me how to cut the peppers and onions and then leave me alone. Unlike my parents or my brothers, he knows that I'm smart enough to figure out how to do the job without cutting all my fingers off.

My father and Bebo have lit up their cigars, the smoke is billowing around my head, mixing in with the thick exhaust fumes coming from the engine. I hope I get a bite soon.

"You feel anything yet?" Bebo asks as he opens up the engine hatch just below my feet.

"No, the only thing I feel is seasick from your cigar," I answer.

Bebo sits down next to the ticking engine. Gasoline fumes are wafting out of the open hatch, and my head is starting to spin. I sit up, shake the rod, and set my feet, hoping that'll make me feel better.

Bebo chuckles at me, as he pulls a dime out of his pants pocket and then reaches around the carburetor. "Let's see if I can make this engine run smoother."

Bebo takes his trusty paper clip from his shirt pocket, wiggles it inside the carburetor as he turns a hard-to-reach screw with his dime, adjusting the mixture of air to gas the engine runs on.

I've watched him take the carburetor apart a hundred times. Now I can see through the greasy metal into the little chambers where the air and gasoline mixture is turned into a vapor, then fed into the piston. When the piston pushes up, it compresses the vapor in the cylinder, the spark plug fires, and the vapor explodes. The explosion pushes the piston down and that turns the crankshaft, which then spins the propeller. It's simple if you can see through metal.

I like being around Bebo because he'll explain how to read a compass or how a complicated carburetor works and never once say that I'm too young to understand.

When Bebo climbs out of the hatch, the engine is humming smooth. He holds up the dime and his paper clip. "This is all El Maestro needs," he says, as he puffs on his cigar then tilts his head to listen to the engine. "It's idling too slow," he announces, then stomps back up to the wheel to adjust the throttle.

We have a box full of tools, but he never touches them. Bebo likes to invent. "I have all the tools I need up here," he always says, pointing at his head.

A cloud of cigar smoke has now settled around my head like a strange gray hat. My stomach is starting to rescramble the eggs I ate for breakfast, when I feel a delicate tug on the rod. I'm not sure if it's a nibble or just the rocking of the boat. I reel in some line and wait, hoping my head will stop spinning.

Bebo told me that some fish will take the bait in their mouth, then spit it out if they don't like the taste. I'm about to call my father when there's another gentle tug on the rod. If the fish has the bait in its mouth and I don't set the hook, he might just spit it out. Maybe I should say something, but I don't. I know the second I open my mouth, my brothers or my father will take the rod away from me, then I'll lose the fish for sure—miss my chance.

Another tug. He's not just tasting anymore, he likes the bait. I jerk the rod back; it bends and strains against the clips. When I try to reel in some line it feels like I'm caught on an old anchor or a truck. Then as the hooked fish tries to swim away the line flies out and the reel whines.

Gordo is the first to hear it. "Julian hooked one!" he yells.

Gordo and Alquilino are already at my side trying to

grab the rod out of my hands, but I don't want to let go. There's something big and powerful at the other end of the line. I can feel its strength shooting right through me like electricity, like the time I stuck my finger in the outlet. I want to pull this fish in. I want to be the hero for once! Why should I give it up?

"Julian, it's too big for you!" Alquilino yells as my father leans in to adjust the drag so that the line will go out easier. Suddenly the fish stops pulling, but the line is still going out.

"Give me the rod," Gordo yells and then tries to pull the rod out of my hands. Everybody's yelling at me, but then I hear Bebo's calm voice. "He's going to run again, Julian. Take up the slack."

I wind the crank as fast as I can, but before I've taken in all the loose line, the fish starts to run and the line starts going out again.

The reel is spinning blurry fast and making strange crunching noises; I can hear the metal clips straining. If the rod hadn't been clipped to the chair, I would have been pulled into the water. The tip of the rod is dipping into the waves; little droplets of water are dancing off the line. My arms hurt, but I'm pulling back.

Suddenly the fish explodes out of the water, not more than a boat length away. Its sword is slashing at the blue sky, the black and purple stripes on its back sparkle as it rides its tail across the indigo swells. "He's longer than our station wagon," I gasp.

When the fish slaps into the water it sends up a huge splash, the line snaps, and I fly back into the chair.

"I knew you were going to lose him," Gordo yells as we watch the tangled fishing line disappear into the deep blue chop. "Papi you should have made him give me the rod; I could have caught that fish!"

"It's gone," my father says. "Nothing we can do."

That was the last thing he said to me on the way home. He didn't even look at me when I crawled into the cabin, and then latched the door.

Keeping my eyes glued to the horizon, I press my forehead up against the glass of the porthole. I can hear Gordo on deck laughing and repeating, "He lost the biggest fish we've ever hooked," over and over again. I'm not the only one. He lost a big one last year, but I didn't laugh at him.

Every time I rewind and then run the film in my head, from the first nibble to when the line snapped, I see it all a little clearer, and then I feel a little worse. If only I had said something sooner, let someone else take him, maybe we would have caught him. But I wanted to be the hero. I wanted to be the one in the photograph standing next to the big fish.

Gordo is still laughing at me on deck but then I hear Angelita say, "Give it a rest, Gordo. He feels bad enough as it is. You don't have to rub it in."

"He should feel bad. He lost the biggest fish we..."

"That's enough, Gordo," my father snaps at him.

Then I hear somebody pushing on the door. "Julian," Angelita calls softly through the slats of the door, "let me in."

I press my whole face into the glass. "I don't want to see anybody."

"It's not just anybody. It's Angelita, your friend," she says sweetly.

Angelita is Gordo's age, and a year younger than Alquilino. We've all been friends for as long as I can remember, but ever since Alquilino started growing little hairs on his chin that look like curly brown wires both he and Gordo have been acting differently around her. Angelita told me once that I'm her favorite now because I don't act weird around her, and we can still talk like normal human beings.

"Julian, open this door! Let me in," Angelita insists. I don't want her to be mad at me, too, so I get up and open the door a crack. "All right, but just you," I say. Angelita steps down into the cabin, but before she can close the door Alquilino stumbles in behind her.

"Alquilino, what are you doing?" said Angelita.

He's standing behind her, ears burning bright red. "I—I just have to—to, um—" he starts and then stops.

Poor Alquilino, he's never like this when she's not around, but when Angelita looks at him or she gets too close, he stumbles over the smallest pebbles and the simplest words.

"Julian, don't listen to Gordo. It could have happened to anybody," Alquilino says and then pushes his glasses higher up on his nose. "There could have been a knot in the line. That's how Gordo lost the fish last year, remember?"

I know he's trying to make me feel better. "Thanks, Alquilino," I say, but I can't look at him because I know exactly why I lost that fish.

"Is that all?" Angelita sighs, and then nods toward the door. I can feel Alquilino's ears throbbing as he stumbles up the stairs.

"Alquilino's a good guy," she says, and then scratches the backs of her arms, "but he acts so weird around me, it makes my skin itch." Then she sits down next to me. "Now tell me what happened."

"I lost the fish, that's what happened," I blurt out. "It was my fault."

"Didn't you hear what Alquilino said? It could have happened to anyone. "

"Papi told me to yell if I had a nibble, but I didn't," I confess. "I should have said something sooner. "

"So why didn't you?"

I look down at my hands, picking at a scab on my knuckle. "I don't know. It happened so fast," I mumble into my lap as the bow smacks into a big wave. The boat jumps and then rolls.

Angelita waves her hand in front of her face. "I don't feel so good." Then she squints at me like she's trying to focus her eyes. "So, why didn't you say something sooner?"

"I didn't want to let go of the rod. I didn't want to give up my fish."

"Go on," she says.

"When I had that fish on the line, it was so strong, it made me feel important. I wanted to be the one that brought him in—I wanted to be the hero just once, but I lost him and now we're going to have bad luck this year." I blurt it out all at once, hoping it'll make me feel better.

Angelita gives a feeble laugh, "Ay, chico!"

"Are you laughing at me, too, Angelita?"

"No, I'm laughing because the cabin is starting to spin." Angelita takes a hold of my face with both hands. "Don't you start moving, too. Listen, people like your father go after the big fish because they're powerful and it makes them feel powerful, too. They don't do it to put food on the table." The minute Angelita mentions food her face turns a shade lighter. "And do you really think your father believes all that big fish, big luck, superstition stuff? If you ask him why his buildings get built, do you think he's going to say that it's because he caught a slimy fish that year, or because he's a great architect?"

She's right. I could never see him giving the credit for his success to a fish. But still, every time we catch one on the last day of the year, another one of his buildings sprouts up in Havana. I have no idea what fish have to do with buildings, but if he says they bring him luck, I have to believe him.

Angelita puts her hand on my head, tweaks out a weak smile, and then pushes off. "I've got to get out of here! I need some air," she says as she gropes her way out of the cabin.

It took every anti-seasick trick that Bebo ever taught me to stay below until it got dark.

My head is spinning. When I open the door and peek out, Alquilino, Gordo, and my father are sitting on the bow talking. I climb out of the cabin and go stand next to Bebo at the wheel.

"Everybody makes mistakes, Julian. The trick is to learn how to put them away for later, keep your eyes on the road, pay attention to the next thing coming around the bend." Bebo never makes a big deal out of mistakes. When the time is right, we'll talk about it, figure out what went wrong. He carefully guides the boat just under the light from El Morro, the old Spanish fort at the mouth of the harbor.

"Are we taking the shortcut?" I ask.

"It's late," he says as he nudges the boat into the shadow of the cliffs. The light from El Morro is sweeping the water behind us as Bebo threads the boat around several large boulders, dangerously close to the dark cliffs.

It's so dark in the shadows that I can't quite see the cliff walls but they feel close enough to touch. My father told me that in the old days pirates and rumrunners used this channel to sneak in and out of Havana without getting caught in the beam of the light.

"Can you hear the sound of the engine bouncing off the

walls? If you listen carefully, you can steer by that sound," Bebo says as he steers out of the shadows and then into the middle of the peaceful harbor.

There are rusty freighters anchored all around the harbor, but the only thing moving on the black water is a red and white ferry chugging across Havana harbor.

We watch the ferry bump into the dock next to ours and drop off two or three passengers.

"You'd think there would be more people coming into the city; it's New Year's Eve," Bebo says and then looks around. "It's quiet tonight, you want to take the wheel?"

I would usually jump at the offer but now I'm not so sure. What if I crash the boat into a freighter? What if my father is right about his luck and the big fish?

"No thanks, Bebo. Maybe next time."

FLYING CHAIRS

The buildings along the harbor, lit up by the streetlamps below, look ghostly, like faces in the dark with a flashlight shining up on them.

Havana is too quiet for a New Year's Eve. Except for the occasional sharp popping sounds echoing off the buildings, the music and the voices all seem to be coming from far away. I'm about to ask Bebo about the popping sounds when I hear Gordo say that they are gunshots, "People are shooting at each other," he says as if he's dead sure of it.

But Gordo can't be right. How could people be shooting at each other on New Year's Eve? It's the best night of the year. My mother and Mrs. Garcia are all dressed up in their best dresses and as usual they've traded each other a piece of their favorite jewelry to wear for the night. Alida's silver bracelets are jangling on my mother's wrists; my mother's golden swallow with the ruby wings is sparkling on the strap of Alida's dress.

The streets should be full of people dressed up in their masks, feathers, and silk, dancing and laughing the night away, but tonight Havana is scary quiet.

My mother is setting out the food. Mrs. Garcia is handing out the party hats with one hand and holding on to Pepe, Angelita's younger brother, with the other. She's got him dressed up in white again.

I feel sorry for Pepe because Alida watches him like a hawk. She never lets him ride bikes or play baseball with us; she's afraid he'll hurt himself or get dirty. Sometimes her clinginess is contagious and my mother tries to do the same thing to me. But I'm much faster than Pepe and I've learned from my brothers how to stay one step ahead of her.

After an unusually quiet dinner my father breaks out the confetti and fireworks and then we run up on the dock to wait for the big moment.

$\sim\!\curvearrowright\!\sim$

At the stroke of midnight we throw confetti at our parents and then jump into the boat yelling, "*¡Feliz Año Nuevo!*"

My father and Mr. Garcia look annoyed. "You're making

too much noise!" my father growls. My mother and Alida look down at the pink rolls of confetti still in their hands and smile politely.

"It's New Year's Eve!" Angelita mumbles. "We're supposed to make noise!"

Just then three sharp, loud metallic pops slash through wood and cement above us on the dock.

"Everybody down!" my father yells.

We're huddled under the table and the only thing I can think of is that real gunshots are nothing like the ones in the movies. Real gunshots are like the roar of a lion compared to the meow of a cat.

I peek out at the men in jackets and ties shouting and waving pistols over their heads on the dock above us.

"We're free! The dictator has flown away!" they yell.

Then one of the men aims his pistol in our direction.

"He's going to shoot at us!" I scream and duck back under the table as the windscreen in front of the wheel shatters and diamond nuggets of glass rain down all around us.

"*¡Viva la revolución!*" he shouts. Then he gathers his group and they dance away.

My father is the first one standing. I hear him crunching around on the broken glass. "The party's over. Everybody in the cars," he says, trying to sound calm. But there's something different about his voice; I think it's fear.

We throw the dinner plates and the food into a basket as Bebo and Mr. Garcia sweep up the glass. My father locks up the boat, and then we jump into our cars. I'm waving good-bye wondering if Pepe or Angelita noticed that my hand is trembling.

Bebo's driving slowly down the Malecón, a broad avenue that runs between the sea and the city. My father is looking out the passenger side window at the dark churning sea.

"I guess we didn't see this one coming," he says and points at the dark gray clouds rolling over us.

Just ahead a big wave crashes against the seawall, and rises like a white-foam hand reaching for the delicate old houses across the boulevard. A noisy crowd has gathered in front of the corner house. Bebo slows the car down to a crawl.

People are chanting and dancing on a carpet of paintings, curtains, and clothing. They cheer when a man walks out onto the balcony, waves, and then says something to the crowd. As soon as he walks back inside it starts raining chairs. They come spinning through the windows, flying over the railing and crashing dangerously close to the wild mob, but no one seems to mind.

My father signals Bebo to keep moving. As we drive away, four men are lifting a black piano up onto the railing of the balcony.

"Papi, why are they throwing all the furniture into the street?" I ask.

"That house belonged to the president," my father says.

"I have a very bad feeling about this revolution," my mother grumbles.

"They're taking back what he took from them, but they'll settle down when they even the score," my father says as the car creeps forward.

"I don't see anyone keeping score. Do you?" my mother asks.

On the next street my mother points out a group of men pulling the parking meters right out of the cement with their bare hands. "Don't look away boys, I don't want you to ever forget what a revolution looks like."

When Bebo turns onto Quinta Avenida, he accelerates. As we fly down the long, straight avenue toward home, my father and my mother are listening to the radio. A man with an unusually high, nasal voice is announcing that our dictator-president has left Cuba. He loaded up three airplanes with his family and all the money they could carry, and then flew away.

Airplanes stuffed with bags of money, chairs flying out the windows, people pulling out parking meters—I'm starting to get this scary feeling that anything could happen anytime, anywhere. It's like the glue that kept everything and everyone together started to dissolve right after I lost the big fish.

I'm watching the little muscle twitching in Papi's jaw, wondering if he's thinking about the year's worth of luck that I let swim away.

THE OMELET

The next morning I get up early and go down to the kitchen. Before I push the door open, I stop and listen to make sure it's safe. I hear Bebo humming a familiar tune to the chop, chop . . . chop beat of his knife on the cutting board.

"Everything is normal so far," I say to myself, and then swing the door open.

Bebo greets me without looking up from the green peppers he's cutting. "*Hola*, Bebo," I say as I lay out a fresh sheet of paper and open up my box of pencils.

"Are you going to make me a drawing of our wild New Year's Eve, Julian?"

"Sure, Bebo."

Bebo doesn't think I'm too old to draw, but my brothers do. They are always telling me that drawing is for little kids, that it's one of those things you leave behind when you grow up, but what do they know?

My father draws all the time, too. Once I saw him draw a building on a napkin, and then after he had his coffee, he folded it up and stuck it in his pocket. A few months later he drove us to a construction site and there was the building he had drawn, rising out of the mud.

I don't know how he did it, but he turned a few lines on a napkin into ten stories of real bricks and cement. That's when I started thinking that drawing is like magic. When I draw I have X-ray vision. I can see how all the parts fit together and then I understand how things work and sometimes how I feel.

When I finish, I put the drawing next to Bebo on the counter. He stops chopping and looks over at the drawing. "Look at that!" he exclaims. "You got everything moving around. The chairs flying out the window, people dancing. I can almost hear them yelling!"

"Bebo, can I ask you a question?"

"Claro, chico," he says as he studies the drawing more closely.

"What is a *revolution*? I mean I know that people want things to change—I heard it on the radio—but why? Why are they acting crazy? Why are they so mad? What do they want?"

Bebo wipes the knife on his apron, then says carefully,

"Maybe you should ask your father or mother. They went to college, they should know."

"You know how they are, Bebo. Even if they try to explain it, they'll make something up because they think I can't understand. They won't explain it like you do—like it is."

Bebo smiles and looks up at the clock. "*Muy bien*, Julian. I'll give it a try." He pauses to gather his thoughts, "Ask questions," he says, and then picks up my drawing. "This is a good picture of a revolution but it's only one part of it. To really show what a revolution is, you'd have to draw at least three pictures. A before, a during, and then an after." Bebo stops to look at the clock again. "But I have to get breakfast ready. The Garcias are coming over," he complains and then starts cutting the onions into thin slices.

"What else? You can't just leave it at that. Before, during, and after—what does that mean? That's how my parents would explain it."

Bebo looks at me like I just insulted him, then he shakes his head. "*Niño*, you're persistent!" he says, and then chuckles, "*Muy bien,* but a revolution is harder to explain than an internal combustion engine. So you better pay attention."

Bebo picks up five brown eggs in his big hand. "This is before," he says, holding up the eggs like a magician about to make them disappear. "Inside these eggs are all the important things that everybody needs: schools, houses, food, and money. For one reason or another a few people have gotten hold of all the eggs and they don't want to share them." Then he starts cracking one egg after the other. The slippery yokes slide out, and then chase each other around the white bowl. "This is during. Things get smashed and cracked, everything gets cut loose, and everybody starts grabbing. That's what we saw last night. It's what's happening now," he says as he pokes at the five yolks with a fork, and then scrambles them into one big yellow lake.

"The after is the important part!" he announces and tips the bowl so I can see the bubbling yellow stuff inside. "You can make a lot of different omelets out of this stuff depending on what you add to it, and how you cook it," he says as he looks over his shoulder at the kitchen door. "Some people are going to love the new omelet, and some are going to hate it. But there's one thing I can say for sure Julian: once you crack those eggs, nothing stays the same." Then Bebo smiles at me. "There's your revolution," he says as tears well up in his eyes.

"Bebo, are you worried that you won't like the new omelet?" I ask as he wipes his forearm across his eyes.

"No, I think I'm going to like it," he says.

"Then why are you crying?"

Bebo is pushing the onions around the chopping board. "Me, crying?" he says as if I insulted him again. "I've got to concentrate on this omelet; the Garcia's will be here in a few minutes. The lesson's over for today. Go play somewhere else."

As I push the door open, the chop-chop starts up again, and I hear him grumble, "Damn onions."

The Garcias were unusually quiet at breakfast. Every time I looked at Angelita she would look down at her plate. My mother fiddled with her water glass, my father pushed his omelet around the plate.

"This is going to be our last breakfast together," Alida finally announced. "We're leaving the country."

Angelita was still looking down, her hair, like a black curtain, hanging over her plate. I could tell she was crying.

"Where are you going?" I asked.

"Miami," Mr. Garcia answered.

"We're leaving tomorrow."

My father put down his fork. "José, I think you should wait. This will all get back to normal soon."

"I don't think so," he said. "We've had a lot of revolutions here but this one is different. Mark my words."

We fell into a strange, uncomfortable silence, eating without looking at each other, thinking thoughts that were too sad to put into words.

Alida was the first to start crying, then my mother. We said good-bye to Angelita and Pepe as if they were just going away on a short trip. We were all trying to act as if we never had that sad thought, the thought that none of us could talk about: this could be our last good-bye.

～◠◠～

This morning a black car and an army truck drove up in front of the Garcias' house, but Mami wouldn't let us go over. When she walked away we snuck up to her bedroom and climbed out the window to the roof that overlooked Angelita's side patio.

Below us there are three men in green uniforms lounging in the shade of the mango tree. It's strange to see Alida's red kitchen table on the patio with three rifles leaning against it.

When a small dark-haired woman marches through the kitchen door, the three *militianos* grudgingly stand up. She's wearing Angelita's shiny black church shoes. They make her old dress look even shabbier.

"That's the lady that moved into Kiko's house right after he moved out," Alquilino whispers.

Kiko lived across the street; his family was one of the first to leave.

The very next day her husband was walking around the neighborhood in Kiko's father's guayaberas. His son followed him around dressed up in a white shirt and red bandanna, the uniform of the new government's youth brigade.

Gordo is sure that they sent them here to spy on us. He says there's one just like her in every neighborhood in Havana.

The Garcias walk out onto their patio carrying their suitcases and then, one at a time, put them up on the table for the woman to search. She tumbles through their neatly folded clothes and then she slides her hand along the sides and bottom of the suitcases.

"She's looking for secret hiding places," Alquilino whispers.

Before I can ask, he adds, "Alida said they couldn't take anything with them—just a little money and the clothes that fit into one suitcase each."

When the woman is satisfied that they are not trying to sneak their own jewels and money out of the country she gestures for them to close the suitcases. But Angelita is not listening; she's slowly folding her clothes, then carefully putting them back. The woman puts her hand on the lid threatening to slam it closed, but Angelita continues folding her clothes. The woman steps in front of her, closes the suitcase and then wags her finger under Angelita's nose. She's lecturing her about something, but Angelita is looking up at the clouds, pretending not to listen. Then the woman points at Angelita's necklace.

Alquilino is leaning out dangerously close to the edge. "That's the necklace I gave her for her *Quinceañera*," he says, just a little too loud.

"You're going to fall," Gordo says, grabbing the collar of his shirt, then gently pulling him back from the edge, as the woman looks up at us.

"I think she saw us," I say.

"We're not afraid of her, right, Alquilino?" Gordo says.

The woman is now holding her hand out, waiting for Angelita to give her the necklace, but Angelita turns away. José gently places his hands on her shoulders and whispers something. Suddenly Angelita turns around, rips the thin gold chain from her neck, then flings the necklace against the wall. The woman in the white dress clenches her fists, but then she laughs and says something to the soldiers. She takes out a notebook, writes something down, and then waves them away. She's done with them.

As they walk to the car Angelita looks up, shading her eyes against the morning sun. I can see her mouth moving, but I can't hear what she's saying.

Gordo and I wave as they get into their car. Alquilino is just standing there, his arms hanging limp at his sides. "I'm going to miss Angelita."

Gordo corrects him, "We're all going to miss her."

As they drive away the little woman picks up the necklace, and then shouts loud enough for us to hear, "¡Guzanos!"

"Why guzanos?" I ask.

"Anyone who leaves is a guzano, a worm," Gordo answers.

The soldiers closed the green shutters, and then sealed them with a red paper stamp.

"The stamp," I said. "Bebo told me that they put those on so they'll know if anyone goes in after they close it up."

We were watching the soldiers paste a big sign right on the front door, when my mother yelled from the bedroom, "The gold swallow! Alida wore it New Year's Eve. She forgot to return it!"

"Don't worry; I'll go talk to the woman," I hear my father say, and then he rushes down the stairs.

By the time we get out to the sidewalk my father is pleading his case. "Señora, please," he says politely, "it means a great deal to her." It's scary to hear my father pleading, almost begging. I've never heard him speak to anyone that way. "It was a gift from her grandmother and with so much going on Mrs. Garcia forgot to return it!"

The woman raises her hand to silence him. "That would be against the regulations. I told you already, once the house is sealed no one is allowed inside." Then she points at the sign on the door, "Read the sign carefully. If you're caught, you can be shot or thrown in jail."

"Señora, please try to understand. If you could make an exception this time."

"Señor, it is you who has to understand. There will be no more exceptions. Things are different now," she says and then walks away.

She is right about things being different. In the last few days, the streets have filled with soldiers, most of them no older than Alquilino. They strut around, carrying their rifles on their shoulders like baseball bats. I think they're trying to impress the girls.

Yesterday I went with Bebo to fill the gas tank in my father's car. We had to wait for almost an hour to cross Quinta Avenida because there was a huge line of tanks and army trucks going by. On the way to the gas station we saw lines of people waiting for the bus, lines for bread, milk, and meat. When I asked Bebo why the people in the food lines looked so grumpy he said it was because they know that the shelves are probably going to be empty by the time they finally get inside.

Of course there was a long line at the gas station, but the

biggest line of all was at the U.S. Embassy. Bebo said that the people in that line were waiting to get their passport so they can leave. The saddest line was the one that snaked around the back of the embassy. That line was for the parents who could not get passports but were trying to send their children out alone. Maybe that explained the steely expressions they all wore like masks. They looked sad and determined, as if they had made up their minds to take the medicine, no matter how bad it tasted.

"How could parents send their children to a strange country all alone?" I asked, and Bebo shrugged. He didn't even try to answer.

On the way back home we had to wait to cross Quinta Avenida again. The same trucks, tanks, and soldiers we saw in the morning were now driving in the opposite direction.

WAGGING FINGER

Our new leader has just launched into his third talk of the week on the T.V. My mother is angry because she can't watch her favorite show.

"No wonder everybody's leaving. Who wants to listen to that man for four hours every night, lecturing, dictating, wagging his finger at everybody." She wags her finger at me. "Julian, make him disappear."

With every click of the knob the screen blinks, the dictator disappears, but then he appears again.

"It's like a bad dream," my mother groans. "Everywhere you turn, everywhere you look. That face—the beard—pasted on every telephone pole and wall. We have the wagging finger, but no soap, no soap operas, and no Armando!"

She used to listen to her favorite radio announcer, Armando, read the novellas every night in his deep, dramatic voice. It was her favorite show.

"*Querida*, you should keep your voice down. Our nosy neighbor across the street can hear everything you are saying, and you don't want to get on her bad side," my father says almost whispering.

"Did you try to talk to her again about getting my pin back?" my mother asks.

My father shakes his head. "It's like talking to a robot. No exceptions."

"My grandmother gave me that pin!" my mother cries, and then storms out of the room.

Alquilino has been staring into space, fiddling with his glasses; he's thinking, trying to figure something out.

He and Gordo are so close but they're so different. Gordo acts and then sometimes thinks about the consequences. Alquilino thinks forever about the consequences and then sometimes acts. He turns things around and around so much that sometimes he can't make up his mind.

But I can tell by the way Alquilino pushes his glasses up on his nose that today he's going to act.

"Come on, Gordo. I have a plan," he says, and then he and Gordo walk into my mother's bedroom. I follow a few steps behind, stopping at the door as they climb out the window to the flat roof.

LOCKED UP TIGHT

Our neighborhood is turning into a ghost town; almost every day the soldiers come with their guns and another family leaves. The soldiers seal the windows with their red tape, trapping the spirit of the families inside with their laughter, dishes, and photographs. Those empty houses, like the tombs of the Egyptian kings we read about in school, are dark and mysterious and begging to be explored.

Alquilino and Gordo have been sneaking out late at night to explore, but they never let me go with them.

"We should do it tonight before the new people move in," I hear Gordo say as they look down onto Angelita's patio. "We can go in through that pantry window, it doesn't have a latch. That's the way Angelita gets in when she gets locked out."

"But the shutters are locked up tight," Alquilino answers.

"We'll just have to pry them open with a screwdriver," Gordo answers.

I stick my head out the window. "You don't need a screwdriver," I whisper, and then climb out to the roof. "Pepe showed me where the extra key is."

"Where is it?" Gordo demands.

"I'll tell you, if you let me go with you."

Gordo reaches for me. "Where is it, Julian?" he says menacingly, as I slip behind Alquilino.

"Julian, this could be dangerous."

"I know, Alquilino, but this is for Mami, and I can help."

Gordo shakes his head. "I don't think he should go. What if he does something stupid?"

"What if *you* do something stupid, Gordo? You're not perfect, and besides I know all their hiding places. Pepe showed them to me," I say, and then duck, just in case.

Alquilino is scratching his chin again. "If she didn't leave it in her jewelry box, then we'll have to search the whole house."

"That's a big house," I add. "The more of us searching the better. Right, Alquilino?"

Alquilino nods at Gordo. "That makes sense to me. I say he can go."

"Fine, but if he messes it up it'll be your fault."

That night I'm waiting under the covers, fully dressed, my flashlight checked and ready. When Alquilino gives the signal, we sneak out of the house, and then climb the tall fence into Angelita's patio.

Alquilino and Gordo link their hands. I step up and shimmy up the column to the balcony, then crawl across the narrow ledge to Pepe's window. Standing on my tiptoes, I feel along the top of the sill and find the key.

The key slips into the lock, the door creaks open and Gordo breezes by me. Pepe's wind chime clinks and clangs.

"Why didn't you tell me?" Gordo says.

"You didn't give me a chance," I answer.

"Shh, Julian close that door," Alquilino whispers as he walks into Pepe's bedroom.

We step gingerly around the plastic horses, dump trucks, and army men scattered on the floor. The sad abandoned toys look like they're waiting for Pepe to come home. The crumpled sheets on the unmade bed still hold Pepe's sleeping outline. It feels like he's about to walk into the room.

We look in Mrs. Garcia's jewelry box, the dressers, and then in between the mattresses. As we rifle through Mrs. Garcia's pocketbooks in the closet the wind chime in Pepe's room clangs again.

"You closed the door, right?" Alquilino asks me.

"Yes," I answer.

"Someone's in Pepe's bedroom. Let's get out of here," Gordo says.

Keeping our eyes on the landing above us, we fly down

the stairs to the dark foyer, then creep along the wall to the door. Suddenly a stooped-shouldered silhouette floats behind the railing in front of Pepe's doorway.

"The son," Gordo hisses.

"Never mind who it is," Alquilino says and pulls him back against the wall. *"Vamos."*

As we dash across the foyer I remember the little hiding place in the pantry behind the tile. Pepe told me that his mother had it made to hide important things.

As Alquilino slowly works the knob, I'm thinking that I could just run back in, get it and run out. My mother would be so happy to see it; I would be the hero. But then I remember the nibble, the tug on the line, the lost fish, and I hesitate. What if I mess it up? We could all go to jail or get shot!

"Wait, there's one more place we didn't look," I whisper to Alquilino.

"Where?" Alquilino asks.

"There's a hiding place in the corner of the pantry. It's behind a loose tile. I'll show you." I grab his arm to pull him back in but Gordo steps in between us.

"He's in Alida's bedroom," he says. We can hear him upstairs opening and closing drawers, jangling the metal hangers in the closet. "He'll come down here next. You guys meet me at home." Before we can say anything, Gordo grabs my flashlight and then disappears into the shadows.

"Let's go!" Alquilino says as he pulls me out of the house.

I notice that the front of our house is all lit up.

"Something's wrong," I say.

"No kidding! Let's go see." I follow Alquilino to the bushes in front of the house.

"Trouble."

The little woman and her son are at our front door. She's waving her arms, pointing at her son, and then upstairs. Then she tries to wedge past my mother and father.

"She's saying something about us," I whisper to Alquilino.

"You have no right to come into my house in the middle of the night!" I have no trouble hearing my mother when she's mad.

"Let's go, she wants to check our room," Alquilino whispers.

We climb the thin trunk of the papaya tree that grows by our window, jump into the room, and as I'm about to pull the covers over my head I see Gordo's empty bed. "What if they come up?" Alquilino is already under the covers, so I grab my pillow, jump out of bed and then pull Gordo's covers back. "Throw me your pillow. Quick!" I line up all three pillows, throw the covers over them. "It doesn't look like him," I say but no matter how I arrange them it still looks like three pillows under a blanket.

My mother is at the bottom of the stairs. "I don't know what your son is talking about. I watched my boys go to bed! "

I grab Gordo's baseball glove from the night table, then lay it right next to where his hand would be—as if he just put it down.

As I get into bed, I hear the little woman at the top of the stairs. "If they're in bed, then you have nothing to worry about, but if you don't let me in I'll just have to assume that my son was right."

"It's all right, *querida*," I hear my father say. "She'll look and then she'll go. Isn't that right, Señora?"

"It's not all right," my mother warns. "If you let her in once..."

Our door opens and a yellow shaft of light slices over Gordo's bed, then Alquilino's, stoping on top of me.

"You see?" my father says. "They're all asleep. Please, I don't want to wake them up."

"Are you satisfied?" My mother taunts the woman. "My sons are sleeping and the real crooks are running away. I can almost hear them laughing."

"We'll see who gets the last laugh," the woman threatens as the slice of light rakes back over us, and then it's dark again.

Gordo grunts as he pulls himself in through the window. He tumbles into the room, waving the little bird in the air as if it were flying.

"Look what I found behind a bag of rice." Then he digs into his pocket and pulls out Angelita's necklace.

"You got both?" I whisper.

"The necklace was on the kitchen table and the bird was right where you said it would be. That flashlight saved the day, too. I was coming out of the pantry, and the kid was standing in the middle of the kitchen. I flashed the beam right into his eyes and then bolted out the door. I don't think he saw me." Gordo looks at his bed. "Is that supposed to be me?"

"Yeah," I say proudly.

"The glove, nice touch. But it still doesn't look like me."

That's the closest that I've ever come to getting a compliment from Gordo.

$$\sim\!\!\!\curvearrowright\!\!\!\curvearrowleft\sim$$

The next morning I volunteer to sneak the bird into the kitchen where Mami can find it. If she knew we broke into the Garcia's house, she would probably ground us forever.

When I swing into the kitchen with the bird in my pocket, Bebo is standing by the stove lost in thought and waiting for a pot of water to boil. I place it in a pudding dish in the cabinet where my mother always puts her rings. She'll think that Alida returned it there when she came for breakfast that last time.

When I turn around Bebo is still lost in the now gently bubbling water, his wooden spoon is hovering over the pot and ready to stir.

"What's the matter, Bebo?" I ask, then lean over the stove to look into his face.

"I'm leaving tomorrow," he says without looking up.

"Leaving, why?"

"Because they're going to send me to school, that's why. They say I have what it takes to be a good engineer."

"Who's sending you to school?"

"The government. The woman across the street told me where to go so I could take the test. I did really well," he says proudly. "It's a great thing. The school is free and I'll get a place to live."

"I guess you like the omelet that they're cooking, huh, Bebo?"

Bebo looks at me for a second as if he doesn't know what I'm talking about, but then he bursts out laughing.

"*Caramba*, how could I forget? The eggs and the revolution." He laughs. "You're right. I do like what they're cooking."

I'm glad Bebo is going to school, but still I'm going to miss him.

"I wish you weren't going! Who else is going to teach me about carburetors and revolutionary omelets? And you said there was a lot more stuff that you wanted to teach me."

Bebo shakes his head at me. "You're right, Julian. There is a lot more for you to learn, but I taught you how to use this," he says and then points at his temple. "So the rest should come easy. I tried to teach you how to think—solve problems!" Bebo smiles and his gold tooth twinkles.

"When I get older I'm going to get a gold tooth just like yours," I say.

Bebo laughs, sticks his big hand out and grips mine tight. "I've been watching you and your brothers grow up. Alquilino and Gordo playing ball, arguing and fighting, always competing, and you off to the side watching.

"I had older brothers, too. I was always trying to catch up, always trying to be just like them."

"What's wrong with trying to be like them?" I ask.

"It's not always wrong; sometimes it's good because it makes you try harder. But sometimes it's not good to play someone else's game. It can make you feel like you're not as good as them."

"I know how that feels," I say.

"Now let me give you a piece of advice. You'll never really grow up until you get out of your brothers' shadows—find your own game."

"What's my game, Bebo?" I ask, and Bebo laughs.

"I can't tell you that, Julian. But you'll know it when you find it. You'll feel it here," he says putting his big hand on his chest.

"If you say so, Bebo," I mumble even though I don't really understand. I bet Alquilino and Gordo never gave it a second thought.

"*Claro, chico.* Bebo knows about these things. You'll do fine," he says just as the lid on the pot starts to rattle.

"*Caramba,* I overcooked the rice!"

Bebo's busy scraping the burned rice from the bottom of the pot as I say good-bye and walk out of the kitchen. His words are still spinning around in my head as I climb up the almond tree in front of our house. Sitting high up on my favorite branch, I can see the beach and the sea, and I can think; it's almost as good as drawing.

ALMOND REVENGE

I'm gnawing at what Bebo said when I spot Gordo walking out of the house. He stops under the tree and looks up at me.

"What are you doing up there, Julian?" he asks, sounding annoyed.

I'm about to tell him what I'm thinking about but then I change my mind.

"Just checking out the almonds," I answer, as he swings up into the tree.

I pick one out, check the color, and then bounce it in my hand.

"They're perfect," I call down to him.

At this time of the year the green almonds are just the right weight and shape for throwing. They'll fly straight as an arrow and if you're the unlucky target you'll feel the sting well into the next day.

Gordo climbs up to my branch and then walks out heel to toe without holding on to anything just to show off. The branch bends as he stands over me. He pulls down a handful of almonds and then points at a street sign across the street.

"I bet you I can hit that sign!"

"I bet I can, too," I say, but before I can get up his first shot clangs against the small rectangular sign.

"Bull's-eye!"

As I'm getting ready to throw, Gordo steps in front of me on the narrow branch.

"Gordo, you're in my way," I complain but he's not listening. He's watching the kid with the stooped shoulders walking around the corner toward his house across the street.

"Look who's coming," Gordo says. "It's the snitch. He's right on time."

Gordo carefully sorts through the almonds in his hand as the unsuspecting boy ambles within range.

"Gordo, what are you doing?" I ask, as he nestles a perfect almond into his left hand.

"You can't do that! Remember what Papi said about his mother."

"Quiet, he won't know what hit him."

When the kid is perfectly framed in a big opening in the canopy, Gordo cocks his arm back.

Oh please miss!

Gordo bites down on his tongue, like he does when he's about to throw a fastball. He winds up and then lets go. The almond draws a straight green line out of the tree, and then smacks into the middle of the kid's forehead. His head snaps back, his mouth stretches open, but no sound comes out. Then his eyes roll like two black olives in bread pudding, searching the trees, asking, "Who, why me?"

"Gordo, why'd you have to hit him in the head like that?"

Gordo pulls me down. "Quiet, don't move."

We peer through the leaves as the boy runs into his house crying.

"That's what he gets for being a spy."

"You could have poked his eye out!"

"Julian, when are you going to grow up? You can't let people get away with things. That's the way it is in the real world." Gordo jumps to the ground. "You're hopeless," he says and then walks away.

"Maybe I just don't want to be like you," I say, knowing he won't hear me. Then I yell as loud as I can, "And I'm not hopeless!"

PORK CHOPS

Tonight my brothers and I set the table. This is the first time that my mother has cooked dinner since Bebo left three days ago. When she finally comes out of the kitchen she's carrying a plate stacked with something that smells like burning meat. She swings the plate over my head, and then sets it down in the middle of the table with a flourish of her hands.

We all nod admiringly at the dark smoldering shapes. My father is the first to guess.

"Pork chops?"

"I traded my alligator shoes for them," she says proudly, and then launches into the story of the pork chops.

Just as she's getting to the end of her complicated

story the little woman and her son slam through the kitchen door into the dining room.

My mother bangs her glass down so hard I thought it was going to shatter.

"Who let you in to my house?"

My father pushes his chair back slowly and then gets up. "How may we help our neighbor?"

The little woman points at her son, leaning into the wall behind her. "Today someone hit my boy with a rock, almost blinded him."

We all stare up at the angry red egg growing out of his forehead. Gordo looks down, trying to hide a smile.

She glares at us, searching our faces for a sign of guilt. "He couldn't see who it was, but he's sure the rock came from the almond tree in front of your house," she says. "But we do know who broke into the empty house. My son is sure now that he saw your oldest son in the kitchen."

Gordo looks across the table at Alquilino.

"That's impossible, they were in bed. You saw them," my father says.

"Save it for the judge. I've filed the papers—I have my witness. Your son will be charged with trespassing on government property." As she speaks her dull eyes range over every item on the table.

"It will take a little time but—" Then her eyes land on the now-cold, rigid pork chops. "There were no pork chops in the stores this week, or in the ration book."

She picks up the burned meat, pointing it at us like an accusing finger. "How did you get this?"

Suddenly my mother grabs the plate, pushes her hip into the door and then disappears into the kitchen. The door closes, plates crash into the sink. When it swings open again, she steps out empty-handed, looking like she's about to explode.

"Magic," she says calmly. "I clicked my heels and my alligator shoes turned into pork chops! Now, if there's nothing else we can do for our dutiful neighbor . . ." She pauses for a breath and then screams, "get out of my house!"

"Señora! It is against the law to buy food on the black market. You're setting a bad example for your children." She throws the pork chop down and wipes her hands on my mother's good tablecloth. "You leave me no choice. They will be sent to one of our new schools where they can live in the proper environment, do healthy work, and start their reeducation."

"No one is going to take my children away from me!" my mother hisses.

Papi wraps his arms around her. "I think you better leave now," he says to the little woman, and then he escorts her out.

"Can she really send us away?" Alquilino asks.

"No, she's just a busybody," Papi says trying to reassure us.

My mother waits for the kitchen door to slam shut and

then sits down. She hides her face in her hands. "She's not just a nosy neighbor; she *can* have you sent away."

"I'm sure she can't—" my father starts, but my mother interrupts him.

"Yes she can and they're doing it already. First they send them out to cut sugarcane and then to a school in Russia where they can put whatever they want into their heads. When they come back, they're different. They won't even know us!"

"Where did you hear that?" Papi asks.

"The new radio station from Miami," my mother answers and then crosses her arms. That's the signal that she's made up her mind, there's no need to argue the point.

Gordo pokes his older brother. "We'll cut cane, right, Alquilino? We're not scared."

Making sure we're looking into her eyes, she says slowly, "I'll send you away before I let them get their hands on you."

"Send us away?" I ask.

"Yes. There's a man that helps parents get their kids out of the country. I've already called and started the whole process. He said there are camps in the United States where Cuban kids can go to wait for their parents to get out."

"You did this without telling me?" my father asks.

"No one's going to take my children away." My mother's face has turned into a steely mask.

I recognize that look. I saw it on the faces of the parents

waiting in the saddest line of all. I look away from my mother's eyes and start shoving the burned black beans around my plate. I never thought my mother could be like the parents waiting in that line, so determined to send their children to a strange country all alone.

~~~

There's a suitcase open on each of our beds. My brothers are flipping through comic books they outgrew years ago; they glance at a page or two, and then toss them under the bed. I'm drawing the angry little woman on the wall next to my bed. She's waving a black pork chop, leading a parade of tanks and soldiers marching the length of my bed. She's the first in line but the last one I'm going to draw on this wall. We're leaving today.

"Hey, Julian, don't you think you're too old to still be drawing on the wall?" Gordo yells from across the room. I don't answer.

My mother used to get really angry when I drew on the wall, but lately she hasn't had the time to notice what I draw, where I go, or even to talk to me.

At night all she ever talks about are the lines. The lines she has to stand in all day to get one signature for our visas, just so she can go to the end of next line to get them stamped.

Every time I ask her about the camps where we're going, she always says the same thing, "The camps are beautiful. There are horses, lakes, and pine trees." Then knowing what my next question is going to be she adds, "And don't worry, we'll be there before you know it." I don't know why, but I get the feeling she's not telling me something and she's not as sure as she's trying to sound.

When I asked my brothers about where we're going, Alquilino looked away and said, "Don't worry, it's going to be just like she says it is." Gordo just stood there with a big smirk on his face like he and Alquilino were in on the joke and I was the one who didn't know the punch line.

When my mother marches into our room, I don't even try to hide my drawing.

She stops at my suitcase first. Her fingers run along the inside walls, slowing down to a walk at the corners. I know she's feeling for the secret compartment she had put in behind the blue lining. Her golden swallow with the ruby wings—the one we rescued from Alida's house—is sleeping in its own secret, blue pocket.

"If I wasn't looking for it, I'd never find it," she says, sounding satisfied.

"It's going to break my heart to sell it, but we're going to need money when we get out," she says, and checks the sides again. "Fifty dollars and one change of clothes is all they'll let us take out, and the government keeps everything else," she huffs. "Does that sound fair to you? How can you start a new life on fifty dollars?"

I know it's not a good time to ask, but I heard Alquilino tell Gordo that they search everybody at the airport.

"What if they search me and they find it?"

"Don't worry, Julian. They won't look in your suitcase. They search the older kids like your brothers and I told you already why it has to go in your suitcase. If they catch them trying to sneak jewelry out of the country they'll keep them here—make them join the army—and then we'll never get them back."

"Alquilino said—" I start, but she cuts me off.

"Julian," she says, her voice rising, sugary sweet. That's the fake sweet voice she uses when she wants me to do something that I don't want to, or forget why I'm mad. "At first I wasn't going to tell you about the swallow—even your brothers thought I shouldn't tell you. We were afraid you might give it away. But I think you can keep a secret."

"You told them and you weren't going to tell me?" I say pointing at my brothers as Gordo glares over his comic book at me. "I can keep a secret as well as they can."

"I'm sure you can, *querido*," she says and then draws an imaginary veil across her forehead. "All you have to do is forget it's there, wipe it right out of your mind."

Then Gordo says, "The real reason she told you was because we might get separated."

"Gordo, mind your own business!" my mother snaps.

"We might get separated?" I ask. "You never said that before."

My mother looks at her watch. "Not another word! We don't have time for this!" she says, her voice dropping back to the hard commanding tone of the last few weeks.

My mother starts checking the new clothes that I packed. "Two pairs of pants, three shirts, and socks, very good. You have to take good care of these, we don't know how long they are going to have to last," she warns.

"Before, you said it would be a few weeks, maybe a month, now you don't know, do you?"

"I'm doing the best I can, Julian."

I turn away and press my face into the wall. The plaster feels cool against my burning cheeks.

"Turn around. I have something for you," she says, her voice higher and syrupy sweet.

When I turn around she's holding out a small plate with one name tag on it. She couldn't just hand me the paper; she has to serve it on the plate I bought for Papi on Father's Day. It has a big marlin jumping out of the dark blue water, just like the one that got away.

The plate and her fake sweet voice are not going to work this time. "I'm not a little kid anymore!" I yell into the wall.

"I know, I know," she says, her voice fraying at the edges. "I want you to pin this on your shirt when you get to the airport," she says and pushes the paper in front of my face.

I read it without picking it up:

"Pedro Pan,
Please Take care of my son Julian.
God Bless You."

"I don't want to wear that!" I say, turning around to point at my older brothers. "How come they don't have to?" Alquilino and Gordo are still reading the old comic books. You could never tell that they're about to leave everything behind, and maybe never see our parents again.

I crumple up the paper and throw it on the floor. "I'm not wearing it!"

Gordo slaps down his comic book and starts walking in my direction. He looks angry. As I scramble away, I accidentally knock the plate out of my mother's hand; it shatters on the tile floor. "Julian, what's gotten into you?" she asks.

I know what's gotten into me. Until this morning it had all seemed like a dream—a dream about some other kid—but now I know this is real. Now, every time she says, "we don't know" or "maybe," she blows a little more haze away from that dream. I used to believe that my mother and father knew everything, and everything went the way they planned, but now I'm not so sure about that. Now I'm wondering what's going to be waiting for us at the other end.

My mother hasn't told me everything because she thinks I'm too young to understand and she doesn't want to scare me. But I'm not too young to know that it's not her fault, and that she doesn't really want to send us away to a strange country all alone, and I'm not too young to feel terrible about it.

I take a handkerchief from my suitcase and start picking up the jagged pieces of sky and sea. "I'll glue it back for you, Mami, I promise."

I wrap up the pieces in my handkerchief and slip them into my pocket and then pick up the name tag.

"I'll put it on when I get there," I mumble, but I'm not sure she heard me. She's staring past me, her face is a closed door.

When we get into the car she turns around and looks at us for a second like she wants to say something, but then she turns away and hangs her head.

The airport is crowded with bored soldiers, nervous parents, and dazed children. When they call out our name we're led into a small room. The man behind the desk points at the envelope my mother's holding, she hands it to him and he spreads out our passports on his desk. He's matching the passport photo to the face, then the name. "Alquilino, Eduardo." I had almost forgotten Gordo's real name. Then he looks at me. "Julian?"

I'm trying my best to look bored like my brothers, but then he points at me.

"Search him," the man says.

Why me? I panic, but I try to keep smiling just like my parents, so he won't know just how scared I am. I follow the guard and my suitcase into another small room across the hall wondering why he picked me.

The guard is a big guy, stuffed into a khaki shirt with the collar buttoned up too tight. His head looks like it's going to explode as he swings my suitcase up onto a metal table. He's looking right at me as he tumbles through my clothes, then runs his hand along the inside wall of my suitcase—right where the bird is hidden. I concentrate on the bulging vein splitting his forehead in half. I don't want to look down and give it away.

His hand stops near the corner. Did he find the suspicious edge behind the blue lining? Now I can't look away.

Gordo told me once that when you're in trouble and can't think of anything else to do, you yell.

"Papi!" I scream. The guard's face flushes a weird pink.

"Quiet!" he growls, as he tries to find the edge again.

Then I yell even louder. "Mami!" the sound bounces off the bare cement walls.

He claps his big hand over my face. "What's the matter with you?"

I wiggle free and jump out into the hallway; he grabs the back of my collar and lifts me off the ground.

"Can't breathe!" I gasp.

Then I hear my mother, "*Ay dios,* Julian!" She's running down the crowded hallway yelling, "What are you doing to him?"

A crowd gathers, and soldiers muscle the onlookers against the wall—no one dares to push back—no one says a word. They watch silently as the two guards push my mother and me into another small room where my father and brothers are waiting.

My father stands up. "Señor, I apologize. He's not used to being searched." He looks at his watch and smiles at the little man behind the desk, "*Por favor, capitan,* our plane leaves in three minutes."

"Getting your children on the airplane is not my department. My job is to make sure that your papers are in order," the little man says, and then orders the red-faced guard to go ahead and search my brothers. He checks the passports very carefully. When my mother sees me staring at the man she raises one eyebrow and nods toward the door. "Julian, why don't you wait outside."

My mother is very proud of those passports. I don't know how, but she found a master forger, "an artist" she called him, who changed the dates of my brothers' birthdays so that they could get out.

I sit down on the floor, put my suitcase across my legs like a table, and take out the handkerchief. The first few pieces of the plate fit together perfectly; no chips or cracks. If I had some glue, you could never tell it was ever broken. But when I put all the pieces together there is still a hole right in the middle where the palm tree should be; I'm missing one piece.

Twenty minutes after the airplane is scheduled to leave, my father opens the door. "Let's go!" he says. I swipe the plate into the napkin, shove it into my pocket, and run to the room. Inside, my mother is checking her lipstick in a little mirror. Finally, she snaps her pocketbook closed, grabs the passports, and leisurely strolls out. She's too proud to let the little man get the best of her.

When my father closes the door, her expression changes from poker face to pure panic. "Run!" she yells as Alquilino and Gordo walk out into the hallway.

We arrive panting at the gate; the propellers on the silver airplane are spinning. A man in blue coveralls is standing on the wing getting ready to close the door as my mother waves our forged papers at the guard.

"Here," my father says as he hands me a box of cigars. "They can't get the good Cuban cigars in America. Even the president is looking for them. They're as good as dollars up there," he says.

I'm not sure what he means, but I tuck them under my arm and look away as he pulls me in. I want to tell him I'm sorry for losing his lucky fish, and breaking his lucky plate, but I can't.

Then he looks into my eyes. "I know what you're thinking, Julian. It wasn't your fault," he says. "This was all coming long before you lost that fish."

Just to hear him say "you lost that fish" makes me flinch. He hugs me one more time, pressing my nose into the scented handkerchief in the pocket of his suit.

Then my mother whispers, "I love you." She kisses me on the forehead. "Take good care of my little swallow; we're going to need it when we get out."

I can tell she's trying to control herself, but I know she can't hold back for long. Her face looks like a big raindrop that's about to burst.

Then someone pulls me out into the heat and noise of the runway. Alquilino and Gordo are running ahead of me into the midday glare. I'm trying to catch up but I can't feel my legs on the hot cement. I'm floating behind them like a balloon on a string.

As we run past the man in the blue coveralls he waves at the pilot. We walk up the steps, onto the plane, and then the big door closes behind us.

As we bank over Havana the broken plate in my pocket is poking into my leg, reminding me that it's not a dream—everything has fallen apart. One minute we were together and safe, and the next minute, everything is broken and dangerous.

Outside my little window the thunderheads are rolling white-cloud boulders into castles, high in the deep blue sky.

Our new dictator can wave his cigar, wag his finger, make people stand in lines, fill the streets with tanks and soldiers, close my school, turn everything upside down, but he can't tell the clouds what to do. Every day, like clock-work, the clouds still build their castles, then they come tumbling down with the afternoon showers.

MIAMI AIRPORT

"We're about to land," Alquilino says. I can barely hear him over the roar of the engines. Two ladies across the aisle are frantically fingering their rosary beads as the tires screech on the Miami runway. Everybody's waving and shouting as if a great miracle has occurred.

Gordo is already standing up in the aisle as Alquilino leans over me. "Julian," he says softly, "grab the cigars!"

When we step out of the airplane, I stop on the first step to look out at the flat landscape. The rising thunderheads almost look the same as the ones I left behind, but then the slap of the gasoline breeze wakes me up and everything looks very different.

Alquilino prods me down the steps. "Pay attention, Julian, look where you're going,"

At the bottom of the stairs a man in a dark suit smiles and reaches in for my box of cigars.

"¡Oye! ¿Que haces? What are you doing?" I clutch the box tightly, but the man pulls even harder. "¡Alquilino, mi tabacos!" I yell. What luck, the first person I meet en los Estados Unidos is a cigar thief. When he realizes that I'm not going to let go of the box, he waves a ten-dollar bill in front of my face.

"¡Dolores! Muchos dolores."

Why is he is saying that? Dolores means pains in Spanish. But when I listen a little closer, I remember what my father said: "They are as good as dollars." Gordo reaches past me and grabs the bill and hands it to me. "Give him the box, stupid. Take the money!"

"Welcome to America!" the man says as he collects the cigar box.

Alquilino grabs my arm; I follow him into the terminal and then stop at a row of green plastic chairs by a wall with framed travel posters hanging on it.

"Mami told me this is where a guy named Jorge is going to pick us up and take us to the camp. Look for a guy wearing a yellow hat," Alquilino says at we sit down.

"Who is that man going to give the cigars to?" I ask Alquilino as I study the face on the ten-dollar bill.

"Papi told me they're for the president. I think his name is Kennedy. He's crazy about Cuban cigars," he answers.

I'm looking around at all the happy reunions. Each traveler searches the crowd, finds their smiling face, then they hug and pull back to get a good look and hug again. I search the crowd, too, but I don't even know the guy who's supposed to pick us up. Then Gordo points at a tall man who's walking toward us. "Alquilino, is that the guy? He's got the hat."

Alquilino stands up. "Jorge, Pedro Pan?" he asks, and then puts his hand out.

The tall man shakes his hand, then slaps him on the back. "Welcome to America!"

INITIATION

A strange city is glittering in the distance as we breeze along the empty highway. Then we zigzag through a maze of streets lined with seemingly identical little houses. I'm counting the lefts and the rights, looking for landmarks, but then we turn onto a dirt road surrounded by a field of swamp grass, scrub oak, and palmettos.

"We'll never be able to find our way out of here," I mumble out the window.

At the end of the road there is a gate with a wooden sign swinging above it. Crudely carved letters spell "C-a-m-p K-e-n-d-a-l."

When the camp station wagon squeals to a stop, Jorge points at the kids pouring out of four metal buildings that look like huge pipes cut in half. "There's your welcoming committee."

"Why are they all wearing bathing suits?" I ask, but before he can answer the car doors open, and hands reach in and pull us out into a cloud of red dust. We're surrounded by a mob, and I can't see daylight, just the pattern on my brothers' shirts right in front of me and an occasional wild face rushing by. The mob is chanting; "¡*Piscina, piscina, vamos a la piscina!*" The pool, the pool, let's go to the pool.

When the crowd begins to move, it feels as if we've been swallowed by a big animal. I hear the sound of splashing water—screams, and then the wall of bodies opens up and there's choppy water below and blue skies above. I take a deep breath, plant my feet, and dive for a small opening in the mass of splashing, screaming kids.

If I stay on the surface I know they'll try to dunk me; we played this game at the pool in Havana. I swim to the bottom, kick off my shoes, and hook my toes into the drain. Above me a tangle of kicking legs and waving arms block out the sky. They're waiting for us to come up but I can hold my breath for a long time. To my left Alquilino is frantically unbuttoning his shirt and Gordo is pulling at the knot in his tie. Brilliant, I think, they're taking off their clothes so that when we go back up we'll blend in!

I slip out of my clothes, and then ball them up. I swim for the ladder, climb out and then start running. Halfway across the dusty space the crowd catches up. We're surrounded again but now they're laughing and pointing at me.

Gordo and Alquilino are shirtless, but still wearing their dripping dress pants. I'm down to my underwear—this is like a bad dream.

An older boy swaggers into the circle.

"Gordo, isn't that Caballo?" I whisper.

Gordo is looking at Caballo—measuring him. "He's even bigger than he was before."

Caballo was in Alquilino's class. He thought that just because he was one of the bigger kids he could push everybody around. That's why he and Gordo never got along. Caballo might have been one of the strongest guys in the schoolyard but the real boss was the kid who came to school with his bodyguard. When that kid was around, Caballo had to jump and dance to his tune. That was one of the reasons why nobody really respected him. The other reason was he was the only kid we knew that chose his own nickname; everybody else had a nickname given to him or her. It was something that followed you around like a stray dog. Caballo changed it and then threatened to beat up anyone that called him by his real name.

"Hey, Caballo. How you doing?" Alquilino says and then steps forward to shake his hand. A troublesome smirk is rising on Gordo's face and somehow I know exactly what he's going to say.

"Romeo, how have you been?" Gordo says.

Caballo pushes Gordo; he flies back into the crowd. When the crowd spits him out, Gordo rushes back at Caballo. Alquilino jumps in between them.

"Caballo, we're all friends!" he says as he tries to hold Gordo back.

The crowd is closing in. I'm hopping around on one leg, trying to pull up my wet pants, but I lose my balance and fall into a forest of dusty legs.

"I don't know what you're talking about," Caballo huffs. "You weren't my friends!"

Then I see Caballo's black leather shoe come down hard on Gordo's bare foot and now it's Caballo turn to fly into the crowd.

"Boys! Boys!" A booming voice parts the forest of legs. "Is this any way to welcome your fellow countrymen?"

Gordo is struggling against Alquilino's grip. I hop over and try to open the knot of Gordo's fist. "Gordo, Gordo, stop. He's not going to hurt us!"

Gordo's temper has a low tipping point; pass that point and he's capable of almost anything.

"Amigos . . . boys," the tall young priest says as he inspects the new arrivals.

My brothers and I huddle together, barefoot and dirty. Alquilino's glasses have been knocked halfway up his forehead, red-faced Gordo looks like he's about to pop, and I discover that I put my pants on backward.

"I see you boys have been baptized," the American priest says in perfect Spanish. Then he laughs. "We are a little overcrowded here and we do not have enough adults to supervise, so I rely on certain older boys to keep order." The priest steps over to Caballo and puts his hand on his shoulder. "I see you have met my friend Romeo." Caballo struggles out a thin pleading smile at the priest. "Yes, of course. I mean Caballo, my trusted helper," the priest corrects himself.

Then someone calls out in a singsong falsetto, "Oh Romeo, oh Romeo!" The buzzing hive of kids starts to giggle. Caballo nods at his helpers, two big kids dive into the crowd and the laughter stops.

The young priest continues, "This young man has been a great help. I don't know what I would do without him! He will find you a place to sleep and assign you a chore— everyone has one. If you behave, do your chores, and get along, you will get two dollars on Fridays and be allowed to go into Miami on Saturdays." Then he looks at his watch. "I have to go speak to the director." Then his face softens into a smile. "Welcome, and please try to get along."

PRIVATE SUITE

We're waiting outside a storeroom when three rolled up camp mattresses come flying out at us.

"Pick them up!" Caballo barks from inside the musty smelling room.

Then, as I'm trying to figure out how to carry the heavy mattress and my suitcase, Caballo tosses three pillows at us. Alquilino and Gordo tuck their mattresses under one arm, but my arm is too short to go around the mattress.

"Follow me," Caballo orders, and they start walking away.

They're halfway down the hall when I finally figure it out. I balance the mattress on top of my head, wedge the pillow under the other arm, and pick up my suitcase with my free hand just as my brothers did. The mattress tips and unrolls as I hurry down the hall, but I finally catch up at the entrance to a long green room. "This is the dormitory where most of us sleep," Caballo says. The two older guys walking behind us laugh, but I don't get the joke.

This place is nothing like my mother said it would be. It looks and smells like the hospital where I had my tonsils taken out. I was scared when I walked into that hospital and I'm scared now. I want to drop everything and run away but I can't do that. So I start counting the metal bunk beds.

Bebo taught me this trick. He said that if you concentrate real hard on what's gong on outside of you—where you are—you won't think about the scared feelings inside.

Thirty bunks on the left side, thirty on the right, sixty times two—one hundred and twenty kids sleeping in the same room. There's a window and a tall green locker in between each set of bunks. All the beds are made up the same: green blankets, a white sheet neatly folded back.

When we get to the end of the room, Caballo kicks open a green door. "And this is where you'll sleep," he says. "Your own private suite!"

I throw the heavy mattress down and look around. "This is a bathroom!" I say, and the older guys laugh even louder. I guess this is the punch line.

Caballo swings the door open and points at me. "I always knew you were the smart brother."

I follow Gordo out of the bathroom. "Hey, Caballo," he yells. "Why are you acting like such a big shot?"

Caballo whips around. "Because, Gordo, there's nobody here to stop me from being the big shot, and you better remember that."

When we walk back into the bathroom Alquilino is busy looking around for a place to put our stuff. "We can put our bags and things in here in the morning," he says, when he finds an empty broom closet. "I'll talk to the priest and see if we can get our own beds."

Gordo is still fuming. "He thinks he's a big shot, we'll show him right, Alquilino?"

"Listen, Gordo, you better try to get along with him. I've got a feeling that Caballo could make our life miserable if you don't."

ANGEL IN THE DIRT

In the morning, Alquilino stashes our suitcases in the closet, and Gordo stacks the mattresses on top while I flush the three toilets and try the water in the faucets just to keep busy. When our things are safely put away, we step out of the dormitory into a red-dust field with four gray metal buildings stacked around it. The only trees in the camp huddle in a clump around a shed, patches of prickly grass grow like green islands in a sea of red dust. I can't decide if the tall chain-link fence running around the whole camp is there to keep the kids in or the dangerous-looking swamp out. This place looks nothing like the log cabins in the color pictures of American camps that my mother showed me.

Outside the fence there is a wild jumble of vines and prickly bushes. I press my face into the fence and say, "I bet there's a million snakes out there!"

Next to the fence, to our right, I see a cloud of red dust rising out of a hole. "There is something digging under the fence," I say. The shower of dirt stops, and a boy's head pops out. The red-smudged face looks at us and then pops back in.

The kid looks familiar, so I run to the hole and poke my head in. "Who's in there?"

I hear muffled voices coming from inside the hole, and then a little dirt man springs up smiling, hair, face, and hands—even his teeth—dusted red by the clay. I stumble back—it's Pepe. But this boy is the opposite of Pepe. Havana Pepe, the pampered baby of his family, was always dressed up in white.

"Pepe, what are you doing here?" I ask.

Pepe considers the question for a second. "Probably the same thing you are, waiting for my parents to come." He rubs his forehead, and a red streak flashes just above his eyebrows.

Pepe watches Alquilino inspecting the opening of the hole. "I bet there's someone in there that would like to see you," he says just as a red hand creeps out of the hole, and reaches for his calf. "Ow!" he yells.

"Angelita?" Alquilino asks.

Pepe winks at us and then sings into the dirt. "*Aaal-quiliii-no* is here."

We're all bending over the hole as a red baseball cap rises slowly out of the little cave.

Alquilino stutters, "An-an-an-gelita!"

Angelita pulls the cap down over her eyes and glares at Pepe. "I'm going to kill you. I wanted to clean up first." Then she turns to us and says, "And what are you three staring at?"

Gordo laughs. "What do you mean—what are we looking at? You're the one that's crawling out of a hole in the ground."

I jump inside and peer into the dark hole. The tunnel runs under the fence, out into the swamp. "Are you going to escape?" I ask Pepe.

"No we're going to use it to go pick tomatoes."

"Tomatoes? I don't see any tomatoes," Alquilino says cautiously, studying the jumble of vines and bushes outside the camp.

"You can't see the fields from here; they're on the other side of the swamp," Angelita says, then starts walking toward the shed surrounded by tall thin trees. "Let's get out of the sun."

Gordo shakes his head. "You have to dig a tunnel first so you can go pick tomatoes?"

"Shut up, Gordo. I'll explain it all later, " she says and turns to Pepe. "Is it clear?"

Pepe scans the grounds. "Clear," he says and then climbs the delicate branches to the flat roof of the shed.

It's our own leafy room with a sky blue ceiling, and trees growing all around it. Angelita removes her cap, then shakes her shoulder-length hair free. "Ahh! That's better."

"Good to see you, Julian." She gives me a hug and steps back to take a good look at me. "You've grown. Pretty soon you'll be telling your brothers what to do."

Then she shakes Alquilino's hand and runs a finger over his chin. "Look at that! The last time I saw you I counted eight hairs, must be at least fifteen of them now." Alquilino turns red, of course. Gordo squeezes in between them.

"Hey there, Gordo," Angelita says and steps back.

"You've grown, too, Angelita." Gordo smiles.

Angelita ignores Gordo's attempt at flattery. She walks to the shade and then lies down on her back. She spreads her hair like a black silk fan on the tar roof.

"Right before we left, my mother wanted to chop it all off. She said it would be easier."

"You have beautiful hair," Gordo croons. He pokes her forearm with the toe of his new sneaker. "So, what are you doing here? We saw you leave with your parents."

"Ay, what a nightmare. When we got to the airport they had given my mother and father's seats to someone else. I'm sure the little woman that took my necklace had something to do with it. My mother said that after I threw it down, she wrote our names down in her little book.

"My father almost had a heart attack," Angelita

continued. "Then my mother called this guy, who helps kids get out of the country."

"Pedro Pan?" I ask.

"Yeah. They had a group of kids on that airplane and they let us go with them because we already had our papers and tickets."

Alquilino is poking at the dried tar with a little stick; he breaks through it and black oil oozes out. "I can't picture your mother letting Pepe out of her sight."

"It wasn't easy for her, but she had no other choice. She made me swear that I would protect Pepe with my life."

Pepe looks up defiantly. "That's funny, she asked *me* to take care of *you*, too."

"You're right, Pepe. We've got to take care of each other. For once in her life my mother was right to worry, because here, the big eat the small."

Alquilino pushes his glasses back up on his nose. "God, Angelita, you're so dramatic!"

"Alquilino, you just got here, and I bet your mother didn't tell you what this place is really like. First of all look out there, tell me what do you see?"

"A lot of kids playing," Alquilino answers.

"Look closer—listen," she says.

On the makeshift baseball field, boys are arguing over a foul ball. In the middle of center field six younger boys are busily digging in the sand. Next to the field, a small pool overflows with splashing, screaming kids. A group of girls is sitting in the shade of a small building, weaving hats out of palm fronds. At the highest point in the camp there is a picnic table with a little roof on top. Caballo is sitting at the head of the table dealing cards out to his friends, occasionally looking out over the fields.

Alquilino shrugs. "Kids playing, that's all."

"I know, there are no grown-ups," Gordo says. "That's it right?"

Angelita crosses her wrists over her eyes. "You don't get it! They're not just playing."

There is something funny about the way they're playing. I look a little closer, trying to compare this to all the other playgrounds and baseball fields that I remember. The first thing I notice is that I can't hear anybody laughing and the argument on the baseball diamond is still going on. We used to have huge arguments but only for a minute or two, then someone would yell, "Let's play ball!" and we'd start up again. Soon we would be laughing and joking around. Here everybody seems to be concentrating and playing so hard that they're not having fun.

"It's like they're playing too hard," I say.

"Bingo!" Angelita shouts and throws her arm around me. "That's one of the first things I noticed when I got here. It took me a little while to figure out why everybody plays so hard."

"So what. We played just as hard at home," Gordo says.

"This is different, you'll see. When they concentrate

real hard on baseball or weaving their hats they can't think about how much they miss their parents, where they are, or where they might end up. "

"End up?" I ask.

"No one stays here for long."

"That's not what our mother said. She said we would wait here until they can get out, too," I say and stick my finger in the black tar. I knew there was something they weren't telling me!

Angelita leans in close to Gordo and Alquilino. "Didn't you tell him?"

They're all looking at me, shaking their heads.

"Tell me what?" I ask, feeling like I've been left out of the joke again. It's embarrassing, even Pepe seems to know the punch line.

"Where are they going to send us?" I ask as I draw a shape like a raindrop with the tar.

Angelita looks at Alquilino then at me. "This is just where you wait until they find a place for you. If you're lucky, you go live with a foster family. If not, they send you to an orphanage. Sometimes they can send two together but three . . ." She shakes her head.

Gordo looks at me with his I-told-you-so eyebrow rising.

"You were the only one that told me the truth," I say.

Gordo just shrugs and then says to Angelita, "They're going to send us to live in an orphanage?"

Angelita stands up. "I don't want to scare you, but you should know how things work here."

"That doesn't scare us, right Alquilino?" Gordo says.

Alquilino doesn't answer. He's watching the older kids who had been playing cards stroll out to the baseball field. They grab the ball and bat, and then force the younger kids off. When one of the younger boys complains, an older kid pushes him down and then stands over him. Not one of the boy's friends dares push back. They help the boy up and then skulk off to a pocket of open space by the fence.

"I guess you're right, Angelita. The big fish do eat the small here," Alquilino says.

"Caballo and the older boys are going to eat us up like minnows if we don't stick together."

Gordo sticks his chin out. "No one is going to boss us around, right Alquilino?"

Again Alquilino doesn't answer Gordo. "What else don't we know about this place?" he asks Angelita.

Angelita tucks her hair back into her cap and pulls Pepe up by the collar of his shirt. "We have lunch at twelve and dinner at six." Then she looks at Gordo like she's annoyed at him. "By the way, everybody is talking about how you pushed Caballo," she says, and Gordo smiles.

"That's not good, Gordo. The most important thing you should know is that nobody pushes El Caballo. He's the boss. He'll get you back, he has to."

"Why?" I ask.

"Because, if he doesn't, some other kid might try the same thing."

Gordo puffs out his chest. "I'm not scared of him."

DOLORES DE LA CARNE

We're trying to decide how and where we're going to sleep in the green-tiled bathroom, when the lights flicker on and off.

"That's the signal, ten minutes before lights out," Alquilino says.

"I'm going to sleep right here by this closet," Gordo calls out as he unrolls his mattress. Alquilino sets his bed down next to Gordo, but if I set mine down next to his I'll be sleeping with my head up against the toilet.

"Why don't we sleep outside?" I ask. "At least it doesn't smell like a bathroom out there."

Alquilino shakes his head. "They have rattlesnakes

here. I read that they like to crawl into your blankets to get warm."

I settle on a spot on the other side of the room where I can lay my head under the sink instead of the toilet.

The too-thin mattress and the bathroom smell kept me up all night. Every time I dozed off, the green of the tiles seeped into my dreams, and I would wake up with the taste of bathroom in my mouth. I was finally feeling my way into a black-and-white dream, when someone came in and turned on the lights.

I open my eyes to the sound of an airplane taking off. Someone is flushing the toilet and there is a hairy leg right in front of my face. The legs belong to Caballo. He's standing over me, briskly brushing his teeth.

"*Molores mis maiting mor mou.*" He rinses and then spits. "Report to the kitchen, Dolores doesn't like to wait."

Gordo gets up on one elbow, yawns, and stares at Caballo as if he has no idea where he is.

"I hope you enjoyed your tile beds." Caballo laughs as he wipes the white line of toothpaste dripping down his chin.

"We never slept better," Gordo says and smiles. "Thanks for asking, *Romeo.*"

Caballo takes a step toward Gordo but he reconsiders, "Keep it up, Gordo. This is nothing like it was at school. Here, I always win."

Before Gordo can answer Alquilino gets up. "Gordo, Julian, get dressed. Let's go meet Dolores." Then he steps right in front of Caballo. Alquilino, as tall as Caballo, leans in real close and looks right into his eyes. Suddenly Caballo doesn't look as big or scary to me. "Lay off him, Caballo," Alquilino says, really low, and then leisurely starts rolling up his bed.

When Caballo storms out, Gordo slaps Alquilino on the back and laughs. "That was pretty good, Alquilino. You scared him. I saw his face."

Alquilino just nodded. He's diplomatic like my father, but also crazy proud and protective like my mother.

We follow the sound of clanging pots and a high warbling voice singing in English as we walk through a big room crowded with long tables. "She'll be coming around the hmm-hmm when she comes, she'll be hmm-hmm around the mountain when she comes."

"This must be the kitchen," Alquilino says as he carefully pushes the door open. Inside a big woman dressed in a faded green uniform is bending over a metal table. When she sees us, she wipes her big beefy hands on her dirty apron and stares at us. We stare back from the doorway, keeping a safe distance between us.

"Well, are you comin' or you goin'?" she says slowly in English, I guess so we can understand. "I'm Dolores, and it's about time you alls got here." She throws three aprons across a metal table at us.

"Them's for you," she growls. "I ain't got time for formal introductions, we got people to feed." We had English lessons in Cuba, but our teacher must have taught us a different kind of English.

When she comes closer, we back out of the doorway.

"Git back in here!" Dolores growls and sticks her belly out. *"Mira, mira,"* she says as she swings her refrigerator-sized hips around in a circle.

I get it: she's showing us how to put on the apron. Then she dances past the table, grabs me by the arm, and ties the apron around me. She pulls me behind a tin bucket brimming with potatoes, hands me a knife, then leans across the table. "I'll bet you boys never washed a dish, or made a bed in your whole blessed life," she says as her pink face floats over a bowl of green peppers. "Raised like little lords, you were. Like most of the kids here you had someone to do all those things for you. Then that mean old revolution came, and now you got to wash dishes, sweep floors like us regular people!" She shakes her head. "Don't that beat all?" Then she smiles at my brothers. "Now for a little history lesson! A long time ago we had our own little revolution here. That's when we sent the king and them other highborns back to where they came from. That's when we became the United States of Ameriky." She speaks each word slowly and clearly. "Here, ain't nobody born better 'n nobody else. *Comprendy?*" she says as she picks up her roller. "Here in Ameriky, you gets back as good as you give." Then without warning she slams the roller down on the metal table, and green peppers bounce out of the bowl and potatoes roll under the table.

"Enough talk!" she yells. "Now, pick up them potatoes and start to peelin'!"

A mountain of potatoes, onions, and peppers have been

chopped and cooked and one hundred plops of "otsmeel" on little, yellow plastic dishes have gone out the serving window but we haven't had breakfast yet.

"!*Dolores, tengo que comer!*" Gordo calls out.

"We eat now?" Alquilino asks.

Before Dolores can answer, a river of dirty dishes starts flowing back into the kitchen. As she pulls on yellow rubber gloves she says, "You can eat later," then she laughs. "*Mucho* later, *muchachos*!"

By the time we finish washing the breakfast dishes and finally hang up our aprons, Dolores is starting on lunch.

"Room for improvement, but not bad for your first day!" she says, as she deals out slices of bologna onto stacks of white bread. She hands each one of us a sandwich. "See you tomorrow, bright and early and *muchachos*"—she smiles and rubs the top of my head—"welcome to Ameriky!"

~~~

One hour before they turn off the lights, we're all supposed to be writing letters home or reading.

Tonight I start on my first letter: "Dear Mami and Papi, I miss you very much. . . ." I don't know what to say next so I stop and draw one of the weird metal buildings on the left corner.

Alquilino sees me doodling. "Julian, quit messing around and write something," he says.

"I don't know what to write. You said I couldn't tell them about how mean Caballo is or how bad the food tastes, or that we're sleeping on the floor in the bathroom. What else am I going to say?"

"You know how she is," Alquilino says. "If you tell her how bad it is, she might do something crazy, like try to sneak out in our boat."

"You think she would do that?" I ask.

"If she thought we really needed her she might," Alquilino says, and I believe him. If she knew they might separate us—send us to an orphanage or a home for young criminals—one way or the other she'd get here, even if she had to swim!

"But what can I say?" I ask and start a doodle on the right-hand corner.

"Tell her that Angelita and Pepe are here, tell her you're learning how to cook, and that they have a great swimming pool—I don't know, just make something up."

"I guess I can tell her about cooking with Dolores."

"As long as you tell her she's nice."

"I *do* think she's nice," I say.

"You would," Gordo says sarcastically.

I write about Pepe and Angelita, then about cooking with Dolores, but that's all. I'm not going to make anything up. In the blank space below I draw Dolores. If I leave out the hairnet that creases her forehead and makes her look angry, she actually looks nice.

GOOD HOMES

Caballo is the first one in the bathroom every morning. He makes sure that he flushes every toilet, and hums really loud and out of key when he's at the sink. I don't tell my brothers that he splashes water all over me when he washes his face or that he steps on my drawing book that I lay on the floor next to my head. If I say anything, I'm afraid Gordo will lose his temper and do something crazy, making things worse for us. Alquilino knows what's going on, he gets up early, too, and as usual he has come up with a simple solution.

Today we got up and were out of the bathroom before Caballo came in. As we walked past his bunk Alquilino slipped in and turned off Caballo's alarm, while Gordo lowered the shade and whispered, "Sleep tight little Romeo."

"*Sí, Mami,*" Caballo said in a pouty-baby voice as he rolled over.

When we get to the kitchen the neon lights are still blinking and Dolores is putting on her apron.

"Well, well, look what the dew dropped in!" she yells way too loud for our still sleeping ears. "Today you can eat first and then you'll work harder!" she says as she lays out three bowls of cereal and pours out glasses of orange juice for us.

After breakfast we work harder, and she notices. When we finish she hangs up her apron and says, "I'm going to talk to that director—tell him how hard you work for me—see if he'll give you all regular beds."

When Dolores came back she looked tired. She put on her apron and said, "Boys, the director wants to talk to you right now."

When Alquilino asked if he was going to give us our own bunks, she looked away and grumbled, "I'm sure he'll tell ya when you get there."

Caballo is standing outside the director's office. He smiles at us as we walk in.

"Sit down boys," the director says and swivels his squeaky chair in our direction. A colorful map of the United States behind his head swells and then flattens in the breeze from the fan. I study the unfamiliar breathing shape, but I can't find an animal or a thing that it resembles. I'm lost until my eyes reach the lower right-hand corner of the map and find the arched back of the green crocodile of Cuba. I find Key West and then hook north, and there is Florida and Miami. Now I feel a little better because I think I know where I am.

"I have good news. I found homes for you boys," he says, just a little too cheerfully. He stands up and pokes at a red dot on the upper-left corner of the large map of the United States.

"There's room for two here in Denver. That's in Colorado." His finger hovers in the middle of the map, then he squints over his reading glasses. "I think this is it. What's it say?"

Alquilino looks up at the map and reads, *"Shi-ca-go."*

The director pulls a piece of paper out of the folder. I recognize the handwriting right away. That's the letter my mother wrote for us to give to the director.

"You're Alquilino, the oldest, right?" the director asks as he scans the letter.

"You, and your brother Gordo?" he says peering over his glasses, "will go to the orphanage in Denver. Now, the little one..." He searches the letter. "Let's see, you are Julian?" he pronounces my name wrong.

"Who-li-an," I say, trying to correct him but I don't think he's listening.

"My name is *Who-li-an!*" I say again.

"Yes, of course," he says, sounding a little annoyed. "You will go to our orphan—" he starts and then looks at me for a second. "Julian goes to Chicago. It's a nice place. They have room for you there."

We're all drawing imaginary straight lines between Denver, Chicago, and Havana. They make sharp, jagged triangles, like the pieces of the broken plate.

Then Alquilino straightens his glasses and stands up. "We go together!"

The director shakes his head. "I'm sorry, but you can't. He's too young for the place in Denver, and you are too old for the one in Chicago. Do you understand?"

Alquilino turns my head to face the director. "*No, el es muy pequeño*. He's little, *muy* little. No go."

The director drops the letter on top of a tall stack of folders. "You have to go," he says and lifts the stack. "I've got kids coming in. Kids have to go out. Believe me I don't like this part of my job." He slaps the folders down and then tugs on the map. When he lets go, North America rolls itself up into a tidy metal tube. "*Señores*, unless you have someone who will sponsor you—take responsibility for you—that's the best I can do," he says and rubs his hands together as if he's washing them.

"*Spon-sor?*" Alquilino asks the director.

"Someone who will be responsible for you."

Suddenly Alquilino stands up and announces, "*Mi tío*. Uncle? He can sponsor!"

"*Tío?* Very good, then this problem is solved." The

director picks up his pen. "Now where does your *tío* live?"

"*En Cuba,*" Alquilino answers.

The director puts down his pen and closes the folder. "He cannot sponsor you from Cuba."

"*Pero*, he's coming, soon."

"When?"

"Now!" Alquilino answers with confidence.

The director gives him a skeptical look and writes something on the cover of our folder. "I will give you time to call, but I must hear from him soon and I prefer a letter. Understand?"

Alquilino thanks the director and then pushes Gordo and me out of the office before we can ask any questions. Angelita and Pepe are waiting for us outside. They follow us across the dusty driveway to the pool and then we sit down and stare into the murky water.

Angelita is the first to speak. "So, where are they sending you?"

"How did you know?" Gordo asks.

"He called you into his office," she says. "That means you're on your way out."

Alquilino looks out over the swimmers. "He wanted to send Gordo and me to Colorado, and Julian to Chicago."

Angelita shakes her head. "That's not good, the orphanage in Colorado is a cold, sad place run by mean nuns. One of the boys I met here got sent there and he writes sometimes. You don't want to go there."

"How about Chicago?" I ask. Angelita looks at me but doesn't answer.

"I guess we're lucky then," I say. "Alquilino told him our *tío* is coming and then he closed the folder."

"Is he really coming?" Angelita asks hopefully.

Alquilino sinks his head between his knees. "I don't know."

I don't like the sound of that. "What do you mean you don't know? You just told the director guy that he's coming!"

"I'm not sure; a long time ago I heard Mami say that her sister and family might be leaving." Alquilino doesn't sound too sure, and I worry because I count on him to know what's going on.

"They're not really leaving?" I ask.

"Relax, Julian. He bought you some time. That was fast thinking." She flashes him an admiring smile. "But, unfortunately, around here that's the oldest trick there is. It might buy you a week or two but then off you go."

Alquilino nods. "He told us we needed a letter from our uncle."

"What if he actually gets a letter?" Gordo says with a devilish smile on his face.

"That's the second oldest trick—the handwriting usually gives it away. He's too busy to check every letter but, if it looks suspicious, he'll send someone to check the address."

Alquilino stands up. "Then we need a typewriter. That'll throw him off!"

"I think it's been done before, but still, if you're lucky it might buy you another week!" Angelita smiles. "And, it'll cost you."

After dinner we meet on the shed roof to plan. Angelita is pacing along the edge of the tar roof, her hands teasing the leaves.

"I know the kid who helps out in the office," she says. "You've probably seen him in the cafeteria collecting the little cereal boxes; his name is Paco and he loves Rice Krispies. He'll buy, trade, and even threaten to beat up the smaller kids just to get them. He's hooked and he can be bribed!" she states confidently. "We're probably going to need around six boxes. Alquilino, you and I are going to write the letter. Gordo, you can make the deal with Paco; you're good at that. Then we'll have to figure out how to get the cereal. Any ideas?"

"We can each save the box that we get for breakfast and then when we have enough . . ." Pepe suggests.

Angelita cuts him off. "No good. That would take too long. We need to start this now."

"What if we ask Dolores for them?" I say.

"No good, either. One per day, per person. That's all she'll give out."

"You can't ask for them, Julian," Gordo says. "You have to take them!"

"You mean steal them?" Pepe asks.

"If that's what it takes," Gordo answers coolly.

"But she guards them like gold!" I say.

"And that's why you and Pepe have to do it. She would be suspicious of me; she knows I would never go in there unless I have to. You have to distract her and then grab the Krispies." Gordo makes it sound so easy.

"It's all set then," Angelita announces. "Alquilino, let's go get some paper." She looks at Pepe and me. "You should go now; she'll be busy starting dinner. We're counting on you guys."

Pepe and I make our way to the back of the kitchen and peer in through the greasy screen door. Inside Dolores is mixing something in a big tin bucket.

"You ready, Pepe?" I ask.

"*Claro,* why wouldn't I be ready?" he says confidently.

Pepe is standing next to the door wearing a dirty T-shirt and the same shorts he had on the first day we saw him, but he looks much happier here than he did in Havana. Now that his mother is not here to talk for him, no one can shut him up. It's like he's making up for lost time.

He pushes the screen door open, and Dolores looks up.

"Pepe, Julian! What are you doing here? You're not working today, are you?" Dolores asks and then checks her work schedule taped to the wall behind her. "Oh, I get it. You came to keep old Dolores company—come on in here."

I can tell Dolores likes us. She told me the other day that I remind her of her son when he was my age, but when I asked her about him she didn't answer me.

Pepe and I sit down on either side of Dolores and then look inside the tin bucket.

"*Que es* this?" Pepe asks and smiles at Dolores.

"This here is meat loaf a la Dolores," she announces proudly.

I look inside at a big pile of pink ground meat that kind of looks like worms. The shiny green rectangles must be the peppers.

"They love it out there," she crows. "They call it, '*la carne de los Dolores*'!"

"*Carne de los Dolores*?" Pepe laughs then looks at me, but I shake my head at him. Pepe just might tell her that in Spanish *la carne de los Dolores* means "the meat of the pains." I wouldn't want to hurt her feelings.

I lean over the unappetizing glob. "Is good?"

"Good!" she exclaims. "Why, John F. Kennedy, the president of the United States, ate my meat loaf and said it was the best he ever had. He did!" Dolores gets up. "I got his picture right here to prove it," she says and walks back to her desk. As she turns her back to carefully take the picture off the wall, Pepe winks at me, I slide under the table, and then crawl to a large cardboard box by the wall.

I open the box, pull out six little cartons of Rice Krispies, and stuff them into the back of my T-shirt. I take out six more and tuck them into the front of my shirt and pants, and crawl back. When she comes back to show us the picture I'm standing behind Pepe so she can't see my lumps.

She wipes the dust off the glass with her apron as I peer over Pepe's shoulder. "This here is J.F.K. himself," she says and points at a man in a suit that looks almost too young to be a president, "and that's me, right next to him, he's got his arm around me, see? I was cooking at a fancy hotel in Miami where he came to give a speech. Someone said he liked meat loaf so I made him my deluxe version that night. They let us open the kitchen door so we could hear his speech. He was talking about how they were going to build a rocket and shoot a man out into space right from Florida. After dinner he walked into the kitchen and talked to the cooks and the dishwashers just like a regular person. Then he asked who made the meat loaf. When I raised my hand he came over and put his arm around me. He said that my meat loaf was the best he ever tasted and he promised that the first American astronaut—the first man in space—was going to have one of my meat loaf sandwiches in his lunch box. They took this picture right when he was promising that he would call me. He said he would not forget; that's why I'm smiling like that. It's not every day a handsome president puts his arm around you and promises he's going to call you!"

Dolores smiles and I notice there's a tear in her eye. When she turns to put the picture away, Pepe looks at me and nods toward the door. I feel like I want to give Dolores a hug because of the tear, but I can't. So I back out of the swinging kitchen door, feeling greasy like a thief. I'll let Pepe explain why I had to go.

When I walk around to the front, Alquilino and Gordo are waiting for me outside. "Did you get them?" Gordo asks.

I pull the twelve boxes out of my shirt and pants and give them to him. Then we walk around to the shady side of the building. "Now I'll go make the deal," Gordo says as he shoves the boxes into the front of his shirt.

"Are you going to do it right now?" I ask.

"It's got to be today. He doesn't work in the office tomorrow. Give me six," Gordo says and tucks the boxes under his arm.

Alquilino and Angelita are walking toward us as a kid wearing thick black glasses walks out of the dormitory. Alquilino checks his watch and looks at the kid.

"That must be him," Gordo says. "He's right on time." Then he steps out of the shadows.

The kid squints into the bright sunlight and starts walking across the red dirt yard to the office. Alquilino slips the letter he and Angelita wrote on behalf of our possibly arriving uncle into Gordo's hand. Keeping his eyes on his prey, Gordo tucks the letter into his pocket, catches up to Paco, and taps him on the shoulder, "*¿Oye, Paco, como estas?*" Gordo says as if they were long-lost friends. I can see him lifting his shirt to give the kid a glimpse of the cereal boxes. Paco takes the bait; he follows Gordo to the swamp side of the building.

A few minutes later Gordo strolls back around the

corner smiling. "Six boxes to start and then six more when he finishes," he boasts.

"What do we do now?" I ask.

"Wait," Angelita says. "We have to wait for Paco to type the letter, then wait to get on the trip to Miami so we can mail the letter, then we wait for it to come back."

That night, right before they turn the lights off, I try to draw a picture of the map on the director's wall but I didn't have an animal or a thing to remember the shape by. So I draw the humped crocodile of my island and three jagged triangles standing on one point: Havana. I could draw Florida easily, but the three triangles remind me of the broken plate, and then I start thinking about my mother. I close my drawing book as fast as I can and then as I slide it under the mattress the lights go out.

"Good night, Alquilino. Good night, Gordo."

Every Friday after breakfast, Caballo pins up a list with the names of the kids that will be going to Miami on Saturday. Those kids are given two dollars each, crammed into the station wagon, and let loose in Miami for the whole day. They always come back with smiles on their faces and great stories about the huge banana splits they ate and the strange people they met.

Angelita says that Caballo is the one that chooses who goes and who doesn't. If you did or said something he didn't like or if you didn't give him your dessert from your tray, you could count on not being on the list.

In the morning Marta, one of the older girls, checks the list then turns around disgusted. "This isn't fair!" she says in front of everybody. "Why do I have to be Caballo's friend to go to Miami?" She looks around to see if anyone else agrees with her, but they all look away—no one says a word.

When she sees Caballo standing by the wall, she shakes her head and glares at the crowd. "Look at you, you're like a flock of scared sheep! Bah, bah, bah," she says, as she pushes into the crowd. That was the first time anyone has objected or said anything about Caballo in public.

Our young English teacher is nothing like the one in my school in Havana. She has long blond hair, smiles all the time, and brings a guitar to class every day.

Because her class is overcrowded, she announces that anyone who can already speak English doesn't have to take the class. When Alquilino and Gordo get up to leave, I don't follow them out. I can understand English pretty well, but I can't speak as well as they can and I like the teacher.

I watch Alquilino walk to the other shaded picnic table where Marta is teaching a group of girls how to weave hats out of palm fronds. They're getting really good at it; they can make them big and floppy or small like a baseball cap with a brim. Marta's hats are the most beautiful; they have swans swimming on top.

The teacher strums a chord on the guitar to get our attention. Then she tells us about the song she is going to teach us, and then patiently pronounces each word for us. I don't know why she picks these strange songs we've never heard of. It would be easier if we could sing the ones we all know by heart, the songs that we listened to every day on the radio and T.V. shows in Havana.

She plays a song about a guy who wishes he had a hammer. No one seems to understand what the song is about but we all sing along just to be polite. In the middle of the hammer song one of the kids starts singing the words to an American song that was playing on the radio in Havana right before we left. Everybody knew it. "She wore an itsy-bitsy, teeny-weenie, yellow polka-dot bikini," he sings in a too-high voice, as we drone on, "If I had a hammer, I'd hammer in the morning." After a couple of verses the song starts to sound a lot more interesting.

"If I had a teeny-weenie, yellow polka-dot bikini we'd wear it in the morning!" We sing as our teacher plays her guitar and smiles. We make the words match the tune and the song rolls on and on, until we have a huge group singing about a guy with a hammer who wishes he had the teeny-weeny, yellow polka-dot bikini.

Caballo and his friends are standing at the edge of the crowd just watching—definitely not singing. When the teacher stops playing her guitar, we keep on singing. She tries to get us to stop, but we keep singing.

I can tell Caballo doesn't like what's going on. He's pointing at us and talking with his friends. He has a weird look in his eye: angry, but afraid at the same time. Suddenly he and his helpers start running around us, pushing and chasing us, trying to break up our happy singing flock, but there are too many of us and too few of them to keep us apart. When they give up, they trot off to find shade, but we keep singing.

As we walk to the baseball field for our afternoon game, I can hear the song mixing in with the splashing and yelling coming from the pool. The girls weaving the hats are singing it best. Marta has organized them into a choir with high and low parts and now the song sounds like something you would hear in a church.

THE WINDUP

While I wait for my turn at bat I'm drawing a picture of *El Fideo,* the noodle, up on the pitcher's mound and Pepe at the plate swinging an oversized bat. The barely human jumble of noodly lines I used for the lanky Fideo look just like the way he moves. I smile because it's the fourth inning and I can hear people singing. I know why they're still singing. This is the first time we didn't let Caballo push us around, the very first time that we stuck together and it was us against him.

When I look up from my drawing I see Caballo and four older boys walk up behind Pepe. Caballo grabs the top of Pepe's bat, pulls it out of his hands, and then pushes him away. Pepe jumps back in front of Caballo. He stands there with his lower lip sticking out, but Caballo just brushes past him and starts pawing at the dirt around the plate.

"Let's see what you got, Fideo!" Caballo yells. Pepe stands next to the plate for a few seconds then he kicks some dirt in Caballo's direction.

Caballo doesn't notice, he's pointing the bat at Fideo. "What are you waiting for?" he yells.

Fideo holds up the glove and announces, "My arm hurts. Who wants to relieve me?"

When nobody volunteers, Gordo starts walking up to the pitcher's mound.

Angelita is trying to wave Gordo away. "Alquilino, don't let him pitch."

"Why not? He's a good pitcher," Alquilino answers.

"You don't understand, that's why he shouldn't pitch," Angelita says and then runs to the mound and I follow her. "Gordo!" she says, "maybe you should let me pitch."

"No thanks, Angelita! I got this one," Gordo says confidently.

Angelita leans in close. "Gordo, why do you think nobody wants to pitch to Caballo? You can't win against Caballo; if you strike him out, you'll make him look bad, then he'll get you back."

Gordo is not listening. "Angelita, this is baseball. It's a game," he says and smiles at her.

We all know that to Gordo, baseball is not a game. Gordo plays to win and he takes it seriously. That's why he's so good.

Caballo was still kicking at the dirt and rubbing the red dust on the handle of the bat. "Sit down, Angelita," he yells. I'm going to teach the shrimp a lesson."

Fideo hands Gordo the glove. "I'm not really a pitcher," he says, "I just like to wear the glove." The beat-up pitcher's and catcher's mitts are the only gloves in the camp.

Gordo watches Caballo doing his batting ritual. Every player has one—usually copied from their favorite major leaguer, a pull on the pant leg, the practice swing, and then the batting face. Caballo crowds the plate and points the bat at him menacingly. "What are you waiting for, rag arm?"

"Hey, rag arm! Pitcher's got a rag arm!" Caballo's friends yell from the sideline.

Gordo rears back, and then fires a rising fastball, high and inside, brushing Caballo back on his heels.

"Strike!" the catcher calls.

"You're blind! That was a ball!" Caballo shouts as he swaggers back to the plate. "Hey wild man, you have to do better than that!"

Now Caballo's choir is chanting, "Wild man, wild man!"

Gordo winds up and spins a curveball, straight at Caballo's head. He ducks as the pitch brakes over the inside corner of the plate.

"Strike two!" The catcher sings.

Now Gordo has Caballo in the palm of his hand.

I've watched Gordo pitch to hundreds of batters, and I know when he gets the upper hand on a batter sometimes he'll toy with them, just to show them who's boss, then strike them out. But I'm hoping that Gordo got Angelita's message; it would be best for all of us if he lets him hit the ball.

The cafeteria, pool, and the shaded picnic tables have emptied. The sidelines are packed with hat girls wearing their half-finished creations, and kids in wet bathing suits. Everybody in the camp has lined up to cheer or boo as Caballo struts around home plate, acting as if he's the one in control of the situation. The only ones missing are Dolores and the director.

When Angelita runs out to the mound, I follow her out again.

"Hey, shrimp, you got a sore arm, too?" Caballo yells.

Angelita shakes Gordo's arm. "What's the matter with you?"

"What do you mean?" Gordo asks, as he sweeps the dirt off the rubber.

"You better give him something easy, right down the middle," Angelita hisses at him.

I wait for Angelita to step back, then I whisper, "Gordo, remember what happened with the almonds!" Gordo looks at me likes he's going to hit me.

"Shut up, Julian. That kid was a snitch—he had it coming."

I grab his arm. "You knew that if they found out you hit

him they would send us all away! You did it anyway, to show him you're the boss, that you're bigger than him!" I yell into his face not caring if he hits me.

Gordo pulls his hat down over his eyes. His left hand is knotted into a fist so I get ready for the punch, but he spins away toward center field.

"They'll send us away again!" I say to him knowing he's not going to listen to me. Why should he? He's got Caballo right where he wants him; it's his big chance to get him back, be the hero of the camp. I understand how he feels.

When Gordo turns back toward the plate he's got that crazy, mad-bull face, and now I can't talk to him. It's no use. I know Gordo, he's going to strike him out.

"They're going to send us away," I mumble.

"Baseball is baseball," I hear him say as I walk back to the bench.

On the mound Gordo is driving his toe into the dirt over and over again, raising a cloud of red dust that drifts toward the plate. The crowd is chanting, "Strike him out, strike him out!" Every kid in the camp, except for Caballo's cronies, is singing and chanting, rooting for Gordo.

When Gordo starts his windup, he kicks his right leg up high. At the peak of his move, he's like a catapult, all wound up and straining to let go. Then his leg drops, and his arm swings around slow, not blurry fast as I expected. Then the ball floats out of his hand, nice and slow, right down the middle.

When Caballo connects, the bat makes a sweet wood on leather sound, and I don't even have to look . . .

"It's gone!" Caballo yells as the ball flies high over the fence, and then drops deep into the swamp.

"Home run!" he bellows. No one else is cheering; the only sound to be heard is the complaints of the red-winged blackbirds rising out of the swamp where the ball fell.

Caballo slams his bat down on home plate and starts his victory lap. "Hey, rag arm, what do you think about that?" he gloats as he crosses second base.

When I run out to the mound Angelita is already there, slapping Gordo on the back. "You did the right thing, Gordo!"

I can't believe it. Gordo gave him a pitch that my grandmother could have hit. He swallowed his pride; he did what was best for all of us.

When I see Caballo gloating and strutting out to the mound I put my hand on Gordo's chest to turn him away and I can feel his heart pounding like a drum.

"Hey, rag arm," Caballo says and steps in front of him. "Angelita could throw harder than you!" Then he turns to Angelita. "Why do you hang around with such losers?"

I stand in front of Gordo expecting him to jump at Caballo, but he just turns his back to him and walks away with Angelita.

Gordo is halfway to the dormitory when I call out, "Gordo, I know you could have struck him out, we all know!"

Caballo walks up behind me, grabs my arm, and squeezes real hard. I was hoping he wouldn't hear me.

My arm is throbbing but I keep my mouth shut. I don't want Gordo to hear. He might be able to surprise us all and give up a home run to Caballo, but I know exactly what he would do if Caballo laid a finger on Alquilino or me.

Caballo squeezes harder, "So, you still think he could have struck me out, midget?"

As I try to twist away my drawing book flies out of my hand and lands at his feet.

Caballo snatches it up and starts flipping through it.

"Give it back, please. That's my drawing book!" I say.

Caballo is not interested in the book, but he must have heard something in my voice. I gave it away—now he knows.

"These doodles are really important to you, aren't they?" He looks at me with a fake sympathetic face. "Right?"

"Yes, it's how I remember and it's the only thing I brought from home," I say honestly, thinking that maybe he will understand.

"Then I accept," he says.

"Accept what?"

"This prize—my trophy for hitting a home run!" he says and holds it up for his friends to see.

I step in front of him and plead, "Caballo, give me back my drawings, please." He steps past me and bows humbly to the curious mob that's just starting to gather. They're all looking up at him trying to figure out what's going on. He looks really happy. I get the feeling that he's really enjoying this and why not? Isn't everybody gathered around him to cheer for him, the victorious hero? But then someone yells, "Give him the book back."

Caballo's face drops back to his usual scowl and he yells back, "It's mine now!"

He's weaving his way through the crowd, heading for the open dormitory door. If he gets inside he'll lock up my drawing book in his trunk and I'll never see it again! Angelita runs up beside him and grabs the book. When Caballo pulls it back Angelita falls. The crowd gasps and Caballo stops. He's wearing a new face, a face I've never seen on him before. He actually looks like he's sorry for something he did.

Caballo stoops to help her up. "Sorry, Angelita. I didn't mean to..."

But before he can finish, Marta, the tall girl that makes the hats, yells, "Only bullies hit girls!"

"Bully, bully, Caballo the bully!" the crowd chants.

Caballo straightens up real slow. He looks tired, as if he's carrying something that he'll never be able to put down. He turns to go, but before he can take his first step toward the door, I hear Angelita yell, "Alquilino, no!" But it's too late.

Alquilino rushes by and drives his head into Caballo's chest. He knocks him into the crowd and then Gordo flies in right behind him. They tumble to the ground in a grunting jumble of elbows and knees.

El Fideo yells, "Pileup!"

In the wink of an eye there's a knot of bodies writhing on the ground. Kids are jumping in and the pile is getting bigger and louder by the second. The last ones to jump in are Marta's hat friends. They're sitting on top, wearing their half-finished hats.

Dolores rushes out and starts untangling arms and legs, pulling the girls off first. I run around the pile looking for my book, checking each kid before they run away.

When Dolores gets down to Alquilino, Gordo, and Caballo, she straightens up and barks, "This party's over, everybody up!" Then she pulls them apart and tosses them to the side as if they were red-faced rag dolls and light as a feather.

Caballo looks around at the kids who weren't smart enough to leave and growls, "You'll all pay for this," then limps off to the director's office. As Alquilino pieces his broken glasses back together again, Gordo tugs on his torn T-shirt. I'm still looking around for my book.

"It's gone!" I say as I follow Alquilino and Gordo to the director's office.

INNOCENT ROMEO

Caballo is standing next to the director, hands folded, looking almost angelic. The director waves toward the two wooden chairs and Angelita and Pepe sit down. Caballo shoots an angry look at my brothers and me. He sees Angelita looking straight at him and he looks away.

Alquilino begins to explain what happened but the director puts his pen down and raises his hand.

"I've tried to be patient with you boys."

"He hurt Angelita," Alquilino says and squints at Caballo. "He can't go around hurting girls."

It takes a lot to make Alquilino mad, but when he does he can be as bad as Gordo—even worse because he has a memory like an elephant. It takes a long time for him to forget and then forgive.

"That's not the way I heard it," the director says.

"Whatever he said is a lie," Gordo yells.

"Romeo has no reason to lie to me," the director says firmly.

Paco, his office helper, pokes his head in the door. "The call from Denver," he announces as if they had been waiting for it.

Alquilino gets up abruptly. "Come on, let's get out of here. He's not going to listen to us anyway."

"We should wait," Angelita whispers, but Gordo and Alquilino are already heading for the door.

Then the director puts his hand over the mouthpiece of the phone, "Boys, I'll have to do something about this. I can't have troublemakers here," he says before they leave the room.

When Angelita gets up, Pepe and I follow, but she stops at the door and turns back to the director.

"I'll talk to them; they'll listen to me," she says to the director but he is now busy writing something down on his yellow pad. Caballo steps forward and signals for her to be quiet, then gently turns her toward the door.

"Maybe I can help," Caballo says softly.

Those were the words Angelita thought she heard him say, but she could never imagine those words coming out of his mouth. She was halfway across the yard when she realized that maybe he could be persuaded to help.

That night, as we eat our gloomy mashed potatoes and sad grilled-cheese sandwiches, Angelita strides into the dining hall and walks up to Caballo.

He waves at the empty space next to him as if inviting her to sit. She shakes her head, then leans in to say something to him. He answers and then shrugs his shoulders. As she turns to go, he gently touches her arm, smiling at her, and motions for her to sit down, but Angelita is not moving. Then Caballo's smile disappears, and she leans in closer so no one else will hear. I can't hear what he's saying but when he finishes, Angelita nods, then spins on her heels and walks away.

Alquilino and Gordo slide apart to make room for her but she walks around to the other side of the table and sits between Pepe and me.

"What did you say to him?" Alquilino asks.

"Don't you know what's about to happen to you?" she snaps at Alquilino and Gordo. "We've got to talk. We'll meet at the shed, I'll tell you then."

As we get up to leave, Caballo is mindlessly shoveling yellow rice into his mouth, his eyes following Angelita out of the dining room.

Angelita is sitting in the middle of the shed and Pepe is standing at the far end picking at the leaves of an overhanging branch. Alquilino and Gordo sit on either side of Angelita. I'm standing next to Pepe when Angelita looks up and nods at him. Then Pepe reaches under his shirt and pulls my book out of the waistband of his pants.

He drops it on my lap and says, "I pulled it out of the pile."

"Thanks, Pepe. That was a really brave thing to do!" I say as I leaf through my drawings. "I don't know what I would do if I lost this."

"I know. That's why I did it," Pepe says and sits down next to me.

"Julian, now you have to do something just as brave," Angelita says.

"What do you want me to do, Angelita? I can be brave, too!"

"Caballo wants your drawing book."

"Why?" I ask.

"Caballo said if you give it to him, he'll talk to the director and then maybe he won't send you guys away."

"What does my book have to do with it?"

"It's called *saving face*. Everybody saw that he had the book and now he doesn't. He wants you to give it to him at dinner in front of everybody. So they'll all know that he won."

"I knew it. I should have struck him out," Gordo says.

"Gordo, you did the right thing, but this is about what happened afterward. You made Caballo look bad. I thought both of you understood. Caballo always has to win, he's afraid if he loses just once, somebody else might start thinking that they can challenge him, even bully him around. It's a sad way to be," Angelita says and shakes her head. "If he wasn't so mean I'd feel sorry for him."

"How could you feel sorry for him, Angelita?" Gordo asks.

"I'll tell you a secret. Caballo is a bully because someone bullied him. He's afraid because somebody, somewhere scared him. All bullies are the same."

"But, Angelita!" I protest and look to my brothers, "It's not fair. Gordo gave him an easy pitch. He let him win."

Alquilino takes his glasses off, fiddles with the tape he put on the bridge to hold them together. He carefully puts them on, but they still sit crooked on his nose.

"If you don't give him the book they'll probably send us away," Alquilino says. "But you'll still have your book, and the other kids will see that someone stood up to him. On the other hand, that might make him even meaner." Alquilino pushes his glasses back up on his nose. "But it's your book, your decision. Whatever you decide, we'll go along with it. Right, Gordo?"

"If it were me, I wouldn't give it to him," Gordo says angrily. "I wouldn't let him win again. There's only one way to deal with a guy like him."

"But if he sends you away, we all lose," Angelita reminds him.

"We might lose, but he won't win again," Gordo answers.

TRIBUTE

I tried to sleep, tossed and turned, then gave up. I pulled my drawing book out from under the mattress and leafed through the pages. By the time I got to the drawing of the three jagged triangles pointing at Havana, I knew what I had to do. It's going to hurt to give up my book, but it won't hurt half as much as getting separated from my brothers.

Even after I made up my mind, I still couldn't sleep, so I stayed up to watch the first rays of sunlight come through the narrow window high up on the wall. The bathroom was glowing its now-familiar sickly green when I got dressed and went to the dining hall to wait for Caballo.

When I see Caballo cut to the head of the breakfast line, I pull the book out from behind my belt. I take a deep breath and then try to walk slowly and confidently. When I tap Caballo's hairy arm, he looks down at me, and I glance back as if I'm not scared of him. But when Caballo grabs the book, I'm sure he sees my hand shaking.

Caballo turns the book over a couple of times, then looks at me, not in a mean way, but like I'm an ant or a strange bug. He puts his hand on the back of my neck, waves the book around waiting for everybody to look up. "I want everyone to know that Julian is giving me this special book; my trophy for hitting the longest ball in the history of this camp." Caballo holds up my book for all to see that he won. A few of his followers clap but most of the kids just sit there with their plastic forks hanging in midair. Then Caballo squeezes my neck, I guess to remind me that he won and I lost.

When I walked out of the dining hall I could still feel Caballo's fingers on my neck; it's kind of a creepy feeling, but I'm sure it will go away, eventually.

So far it seems as if it was worth it. Since I gave him my book, Caballo hasn't bothered anybody. For now he doesn't seem to be interested in what we're doing and he hasn't noticed that everybody is whispering about what happened with me and the book. The girls weaving the hats have not stopped arguing about whether or not I should have given up my book. They all agree that Caballo has hit a new high—or low, depending how you look at it—on the bully scale.

Every time they ask me how I feel about giving up my book, I answer the same way, "I don't want to talk about it. I just want to forget it!" Then I get the same nervous feeling in my stomach.

I know that if Caballo hears even a snippet of what they're saying about him, he'll have to do something to show us he's boss again. Bebo always said that you should listen to your stomach.

All week Caballo has been staying at the fringes of things, like he's just one of us. But today, Friday, after dinner, he came forward and tacked up the list for the Saturday-morning trip to Miami.

Pepe and I worm our way under and around the kids gathered in front of the list. When we get next to the wall we stand up at the same time and scan the list. "Alquilino and Gordo are on the list!" we say at exactly the same time. My stomach starts to hurt.

"Something is wrong here," I mumble as we crawl back to where Alquilino, Gordo, and Angelita are standing.

Angelita looks at me and asks, "What's the matter, Julian?"

"Alquilino and Gordo are on the list," I say to Angelita.

"What's wrong with that? We gave him what he wanted; now he's giving us something back. That's the way it works," Angelita says. "Maybe he's not such a bad guy."

"Why aren't we all on the list?" I ask as Alquilino and Gordo crowd around me.

"I wouldn't worry about it, Julian," Angelita answers, leaning over Alquilino's right shoulder. "A lot of other kids want to go on that trip."

I look at Alquilino and notice his ears are turning a bright shade of red. Angelita has draped one arm over his shoulder.

"Ma-maybe Angelita's right," he barely manages to blubber out. I don't know why but whenever she gets that close to him his brain just turns to mush. I turn to Gordo; I can always rely on him for the blunt truth.

"What do you think, Gordo?"

"What do I think?" he says as he watches Alquilino and Angelita out of the corner of his eye. "I think it's going to be great to get out of this place, even if it's just for a day."

DID YOU SAY GOOD-BYE?

It's early Saturday morning and I'm watching a rectangle of sunlight creep up the green-tile wall. I'm too nervous to stay in bed, so I roll up my mattress, get dressed, and walk out past the other sleeping campers. The camp station wagon is already parked in front of the dormitory; its rear gate is open and Caballo is tossing a red blanket into the back. The other kids going on the trip are starting to stumble out the door; they mill around to let Caballo know they're up and head for the cafeteria to get breakfast. I walk back to the bathroom, gently pushing the door open so it won't make any noise, but when I look inside, Alquilino and Gordo are already up, both wearing clean shirts. We stack the three blue suitcases one on top of the other so they'll fit in the closet and then head for the cafeteria.

Caballo and one of his helpers are standing by the door of the dormitory as we walk out. Last night I tried to tell Alquilino and Gordo about the feeling in my stomach, but they just laughed at me and said that they knew what they were doing.

"Make sure you get some breakfast before you go. It's a long day," Caballo says with a strange smile on his face.

"He's up to something," I whisper to Alquilino, but he just nods and walks out into the morning sun. He's not too talkative in the morning.

Gordo and Alquilino walk into the cafeteria ahead of me. Before I go in I look back and see Caballo standing alone by the door. When he sees me looking at him he waves me toward the cafeteria door. "Go have your breakfast!" he yells and smiles again.

After breakfast we walk out of the cafeteria and there's Caballo standing by the back of the car holding his clipboard. When he sees us he says something to his helper, who slams the back gate closed.

As Gordo slides into the backseat next to Alquilino, he looks at me and shakes his head. "If you could see your face right now." He laughs. "Hey, Alquilino, I know what it is," Gordo says. "He's afraid to be without his big brothers."

"We'll bring you something back. Don't worry, Julian," Alquilino says right before Gordo closes the door.

Caballo signals to the driver and the station wagon

pulls away, a cloud of red dust rising up behind it as it picks up speed. When it turns to go through the gate the cloud shifts and I think I see a familiar blue color peeking out from under the red blanket in the back of the station wagon. Our suitcases are the same shade of blue. I run after them trying to get a better look, but the swirling curtain of dust blocks my view. I keep running until the cloud and the car disappear out by the paved road.

As I walk back toward the camp, the gray metal buildings look even stranger than they did the first time I saw them: the distances seem bigger, emptier. I feel like there is nothing keeping the wind from picking me up and blowing me over the chain-link fence along with the red dust.

"You're not alone, you know," I hear Pepe say behind me.

TOMA-TRON

Angelita is waiting in the shade of the building closest to the fence. When she sees us, she calls out, "Hurry up, Julian, we've got things to do. Don't worry; Alquilino and Gordo will be back by dinnertime."

I nod and follow Angelita and Pepe out to the fence.

"Pepe?" she says as Pepe looks around to see if anyone's watching. "Clear," he says.

Angelita sweeps away a pile of dried leaves, lifts up the trap door covering their tunnel, and points into the garbage can–sized hole. Pepe jumps in first, then she points at me. "Get in, before anyone sees us."

Pepe looks like a big rodent in shorts as he scurries ahead of me in the dark narrow tunnel.

"Where are we going?" I ask.

"Shh." I hear Angelita behind me.

Then Pepe stops. He stands up and the light streams in. Angelita whispers, "When you climb out, run as fast as you can into the reeds."

We squeeze out of the tunnel. Angelita drops the trap door, and then carefully covers it with dirt.

"Where are we?" I ask, but they're already running ahead of me. As they disappear into a stand of reeds growing in brackish water, Pepe calls back to me, "Watch out for snakes!"

"Snakes?"

I follow them into the reeds, jumping from one clump of grass to another, holding my arms out for balance just like Pepe. I'm just starting to get the hang of it when I hear Angelita say, "This is where we saw the alligator the other day!" That's when I lose my concentration, miss the next clump, and fall through a curtain of cattails.

When I drag myself out of the reeds Angelita and Pepe are waiting for me at the edge of a big open field with rows of tomato plants receding into the trees.

"I bet you thought we were running away," Pepe says, before I have a chance to ask.

"It's always good to make a little money," Angelita says and leads the way to a cluster of trees where a dark-haired woman is standing by a stack of bushels. She hands us each one, copies its number into a ledger, and nods toward the field. "Row eleven," she says as the sound of an engine sputtering and coughing behind a shed almost drowns her out. I think of how Bebo could have that engine running smooth as silk in no time at all.

We walk out into the sun carrying our bushels past dozens of men and women stooped over the tomato plants. Their broad straw hats hide their faces, but I can see their hands dancing into the vines, gently twisting, pulling, then carefully placing each tomato into the bushels.

When we get to row eleven, I start picking the delicate fruit, trying to imitate the twist and pull. It looks easier than it is.

The pickers are talking about the meals their families will eat, the roof that will be fixed, and debts they'll pay off with the money they send home. All the while someone has been singing the same song, over and over.

"Two dollars a basket, three baskets a day, seven days a week."

"Seven days a week. Forty-two dollars!"

Now the midday sun is stinging the back of my neck and when I stand up my head starts spinning. I drop down on my knees.

"Are you all right?" Pepe asks.

I feel light-headed and hungry. "Yeah, sure. I just dropped one."

Angelita helps me up on my feet. "I wanted you to see this, Julian. So that when you start feeling sorry for yourself you've got something to compare your troubles to. These people are here alone, too, but they have to work seven days a week, for forty-two dollars! That's just enough to live on, but they still send money home. They get tired and lonely, but they just swallow it and keep going. They have to." She looks at me, to make sure I get the point, then gets up. "Let's take the bushels in," she says, and we start walking toward the shed. "Before you and your brothers arrived, Pepe and I used to come here a lot. The very first time Pepe saw this, he stopped acting like a spoiled little brat."

"I was never a brat," Pepe complains.

"That's a matter of opinion," Angelita says and pushes both of us into the shade. "Let's turn our bushels in. I'll buy the sandwiches."

The dark-haired woman is now behind the shed standing next to a three-sided wooden box that seems to be bouncing on its own. Pepe and Angelita tip their bushels into the box; the woman examines the tomatoes, deftly picking out the bruised ones, and then herding the rest through the open side. A rolling conveyor belt, made of rubber doormats joined by links of metal wire bounces the chosen ones happily along until they are gently dropped into a shaking frame of wire mesh. They jump like red-faced children on their wire trampoline. Then one by one the smaller ones drop through openings in the wire and roll left on a tin funnel to a basket, the larger ones roll to the right.

A tall skinny guy, just a little older than Alquilino, walks up and stands right next to me.

"I call it the Toma-Tron!" he announces proudly, as I walk closer to inspect the amazing clicking, squeaking machine.

"I made the whole thing out of stuff that I found lying around," he says and beats on the fender of a rusty black truck raised up on cement blocks. "I pulled this truck out of a ditch." He leans into the cab to adjust a brick resting on the accelerator. The engine speeds up and the long rubber belt, stitched together out of inner tubes, spins faster around the metal rim of the right rear tire. I bend down to follow the rubber belt spinning under the Toma-Tron. I can recognize every part. There's a wheel from a baby carriage, chrome racks from a refrigerator, chain and sprocket from a bicycle. Each part had another use, another life, but the way he fit one to the other they look like they've always belonged together. I wish Bebo were here to see this.

"That's an amazing thing!" I say as I straighten up.

He pokes his hand in my direction. "I am Tomás, inventor-mechanic."

"I'm Julian. Artist and, I guess, tomato picker."

Tomás laughs and pumps my hand. *"¿Un hermano, Cubano?"*

"How did you know?"

"We've got Mexicans, Ecuadorians, Guatemalans here. We all speak the same language but just a little different. It's as if our tongues are bent and shaped by the mountain, river, or sea we grew up next to."

When Angelita and Pepe come back they have three sandwiches wrapped in crinkled wax paper. Angelita pats Tomás on the back. "Hey, Tomás, are you bragging about your Toma-Tron again?"

"Angelita, Pepe, *Pedro Paneros,* good to see you again. Will you join me for lunch?"

We sit down under a tree with silver roots that look like big snakes slithering in and out of the ground. Tomás reaches under one and pulls out a big yellow purse made of quilted plastic leather.

"Best lunch box I've ever had," he says. "It's waterproof—keeps things nice and cold." He pulls out a milk bottle filled with a cloudy green liquid with ice cubes clinking in it.

"Tomás-ade. People say it's the most refreshing drink in all Miami. Try it!" Tomás fills a dented metal cup, and then passes it to me. At first I take a polite sip, but then I gulp the rest. "Wow, that's good." I exclaim as I shamelessly hold the empty cup out for a refill. "What's in it?"

"Oranges that roll off the big trucks as they leave the groves; the limes come from a little orphaned tree down by the river, then I sweeten it with the little packets of sugar that Pirate Angel gives away. But that's just what's in it. What makes it good is the inspiration," Tomás claims as he caps the bottle.

"If you keep selling your inspiration for a nickel a glass along with these sandwiches, you're going to be a millionaire by next year," Angelita says.

"I don't care about being a millionaire. I'm just trying to make enough money to fix up my boat."

"What kind of boat do you have?" I ask.

"The kind that doesn't float!" Pepe snickers.

"Pepe is right; she doesn't float yet, but she will soon!"

"Where is it?" I ask.

"Down by the river, under the highway." Tomás laughs.

Suddenly the old truck engine sputters, the Toma-Tron jumps, and tomatoes bounce out into the sun. Tomás packs away his lunch and then runs over to the conveyor belt. I walk over to the truck, climb up on the fender, and check out the carburetor. This engine is a little different from the one in our boat, but the parts are all in the same place. So I take out a dime and reach in. I try not to touch any of the hot parts as I feel around for the hidden screw in the back of the carburetor. "Here it is," I say. Half a turn clockwise makes it run even rougher, but one turn counterclockwise and the engine runs smooth. I fine-tune the carburetor by listening and adjusting the screw a hair this way and a tap that way.

"How did you do that?" asks Tomás.

I hold up my dime. "There's a little screw tucked in there; you can't reach it with a regular screwdriver," I say, trying to sound matter-of-fact about it.

"I can't ever get it to run that smooth," he says and then smiles at me. "You've got a good ear for this. I could use a good engine man on my boat."

Just then the dark-haired lady calls out, "Tomás, the little tomatoes are bouncing into the wrong bucket! "

"Oops, I got to go. Nice to meet you, Julian artist-mechanic. Come down to the river, check out my boat. Angelita has a map, and it's not as bad as Pepe says." Tomás slaps him on the back and bows to Angelita. "Till the next time we meet."

We manage to pick one more bushel full, drag it back to the shade, and the lady with the black hair checks her ledger and counts out six dollars.

"You can go first on the way back," Pepe offers. When we get to the other end of the tunnel I push up on the trapdoor, but it will not budge. Angelita squeezes in beside me. "One, two." We both push; the trapdoor rises just a few inches and then comes down again.

Then we hear Caballo's muffled voice. "Have a good day at the tomato fields?"

"It's Caballo," Angelita whispers.

"What does he want?" I ask.

"I don't remember giving anybody permission to dig a tunnel or to leave the camp. The fine for breaking this rule is three dollars."

"That's half of what we made," I mumble to Pepe.

"Hand it over before I get mad," Caballo insists.

"Why do we have to pay you?" I say.

"Is that the smart brother?" he says in a mocking tone, that even all the dirt between us can't soften. "You pay me because you broke my rules," Caballo states as if he's tired of repeating it.

We're packed in tight, the walls are squeezing in on us,

and I can't breathe. "I got to get out!" I yell, and then push against the door with all my might. The trapdoor raises just enough to let some air in. I hear a sandy scuffling sound as I stick my hand out.

"Hey!" Caballo shouts as he scrambles off the hatch, and then his foot comes down hard on my fingers.

"Ow!" I cry and try to pull my hand back. "You're stepping on my hand!"

"It's not my fault. You threw me off balance."

My hand hurts. I'm trapped, and I can't catch my breath.

"My head's going to explode!" I yell into the dirt. Something is scrambling, scratching around in my chest. It feels like an angry little animal that's been cooped up for a long time and now it has to get out.

"I already gave you my book. I'm not paying!" I scream into Pepe's ear. I've been angry before, but this feeling is different, and it's bubbling over. "I'm going to get you back, Caballo!"

"Shut up, Julian," Angelita says as she digs into her pocket, pulls out her two dollars, and then gives it to Pepe. It's not right for them to pay for me, so I wiggle on my side and grab one of my bills with my free hand, then slide it out.

"Gordo was right," I yell. "If you keep giving in, he'll keep on pushing us around!"

"What are you going to do about it?"

"I'm going to tell my brothers! We'll get you back."

Angelita punches me on the arm, "Shut up, Julian."

"Tell your brothers?" I hear him laugh as his hand scoops up the bills from the dirt. "They can't help you now, smart boy," he says as he walks away.

"Angelita, did you hear what he said?"

"I don't know, Julian, everything sounds muffled in here. But I do know that you can't fight with him—he makes the rules and he always wins."

"I've got to find my brothers!"

I push the trapdoor off and crawl out of the hole. My hand is still throbbing as I run past the ball fields and the pool, and then I see the dusty station wagon parked in front of the director's door. Good, they're back. I hurry through the dormitory, then slam into the bathroom. I knew it!

My shirts, pants, and underwear are scattered all over the floor with a big red footprint stamped on each one, my suitcase is lying open on its side. The closet where we stored our suitcases is open and empty. Alquilino and Gordo are gone.

I should have done something—I should have made them listen to me.

I'm walking out of the bathroom, looking down at the tiles when I run into a plaid-shirt wall. I look up to see Caballo towering over me. He's too big, too close, and I can't remember a single one of the things I imagined telling him to his face. The best I can do is to squeak, "I gave you my book."

"I gave you my book," he mocks, in an even higher, squeakier voice than mine.

The new bubbling anger is rising again. Maybe I can kick him and run away. I try but my leg feels like it belongs to someone else. Again, the best I can do is to dig my toe into the ground, sending a clod of red dirt flying in his direction.

Caballo grabs my arm with his baseball mitt–sized hand, squeezes really hard, and then growls, "Don't you ever try that again." Caballo's free hand is hanging in front of my face. I picture it crushing my head like it was a boiled egg.

"You're lucky nobody saw that," he says out of the side of his mouth as he looks around. Then he squeezes my arm even harder and pushes me down to the ground. "I'm going to let you off easy this time," he says. I can hear him laughing as he walks away.

When the fear finally drains out of my legs, I get up and make my way to the shed. I hide out on the roof, drawing on a piece of paper I've been carrying around in my back pocket since I lost my book to Caballo. I draw myself trembling and smaller than I actually am. I'm ashamed of myself for getting so scared, letting him push me around. If Alquilino and Gordo had seen me, I'm sure they would have laughed, too.

BIG SNAKE

My brothers weren't the only ones to leave today. I guess that's why I don't have to sleep in the bathroom anymore. It's late but I'm awake in my new bunk drawing by the light of the moon. I'm afraid to stop drawing. Every time I put my pencil down, my thoughts get jumbled up. I get sad and angry at the same time.

The drawing that I did this afternoon is on the other side of the paper. I didn't want to look at it but it's whispering through, reminding me.

Bebo tried to teach me about being scared too. He said it's just like when you make a mistake, you can't dwell on it. The trick is to focus past the scary thing and to pay attention to the next thing. He also told me that some people can smell fear just like dogs can. If they know you're afraid it makes it easier for them to push you around.

I knew all that stuff before Caballo scared me today, but it didn't help. I have to figure out how Bebo's trick works so I can keep my brain from freezing up.

On this side of the page I draw myself bigger than the ghost of scared me from the other side. Using firm clear lines I make rays shooting out of my eyes and Caballo's back as he runs away.

Maybe next time I get scared, I'll be the only one that knows it.

The dormitory is much noisier than the bathroom. I hear a boy calling for his mother in his sleep. I put my pencil down and listen to his muffled sobs echo off the metal walls. No matter how big I draw myself, I still feel really small in this big dark room. But I'm not going to cry; Caballo might hear me.

Outside, the clouds part and a beam of moonlight glows on the screen. I climb down from my bunk and stare out beyond the fence into the spooky night.

"Big," I gasp as something black and as thick as an inner tube starts climbing up the other side of the screen right in front of me.

Then I hear a voice behind me. "There are even bigger ones in the swamp." I turn around and there's Angelita.

"What're you doing here?" I ask, as she leans in close to inspect the snake.

"I couldn't sleep, either," she says and then runs her

finger along its yellowy underside. "I hope you're not still mad at me for giving Caballo the money."

"I was," I say and look away.

"I never saw you that mad. He wants to make you mad, so he can squash you like a bug."

"I know that, Angelita."

"You should have given him the money when he asked for it. "

"That's not right. We worked for that money. He took my book and sent Alquilino and Gordo away!"

"Shh! You're going to wake everybody up. Let's go outside," she says and I follow her past the snoring, mumbling sleepers.

Outside, the moon is hanging low over the swamp as if it's caught on the spikes of the chain-link fence. There are things moving in the bushes, probably big animals hunting the little ones in the dark.

"I come out here a lot to think," Angelita says.

"What do you think about?"

"My old friends, my parents, eating mangoes in the trees—you know, things I shouldn't think about because they make me sad." Angelita sighs and sits down. I sit down next to her.

"I have the same problem but now I have two more people I can't think about," I say and pull out a clump of grass.

"Julian, it's terrible that they split you up, but you're not alone here; you still have me and Pepe."

"I'm worried about Alquilino and Gordo. The other day at the baseball field they were talking about all the places they can send you, and Fideo kept saying that the very worst one was the one in Denver—the one they sent my brothers to. Fideo said they have older kids there that make Caballo look like an angel."

"I wouldn't worry too much about them. You know how they are. Alquilino and Gordo always stick together. They'll take care of each other."

"Angelita, we have to tell the director about Caballo."

"We did already. He thinks he needs Caballo to keep everybody in line. This place is overcrowded and he doesn't have enough help. He's afraid of losing control again. He doesn't want to hear anything about how Caballo does the job, as long as he gets it done."

"But, he took our money and my book and stepped on my hand! We should tell him, maybe he'll listen now," I say, trying to keep my voice down.

"I don't think he's in the mood to listen to us now," Angelita says, then pulls an envelope out of her pocket and drops it on my lap. "This look familiar to you?"

There's a big red *X* slashed across the address but I can still read it. I'm holding the fake letter from our uncle.

"Caballo gave it to me after you ran off. He said he had talked the director into waiting to send your brothers away but then this came back in Wednesday's mail. The director checked it out, and when he found out it was a fake, he hit the roof. Caballo said that he was so mad that he bumped two other kids off just to put Alquilino and Gordo on the next flight out. It was weird." Angelita stops and looks at her hands.

"What's weird?" I ask.

"I got the feeling that Caballo was actually trying to let me know that he tried. It was weird, because I think he was apologizing."

"He likes you. You're the only person in this whole camp that could actually feel sorry for him."

"I don't know, I just think he's the saddest, loneliest person in the world."

"Angelita, he might be lonely and sad but he's still a mean person. He enjoys scaring people. He even picks on little kids."

"But there's a reason why," Angelita says.

"It doesn't matter! He still does it. If the director won't help us, we have to fight back or he'll get worse. I think Gordo was right."

"Caballo's too big to fight," Angelita says and looks off into the dark. "The way I look at it we have two choices. We can either make believe that we don't mind being pushed around, or we can think our way around the problem— learn how to handle him," she says and then strides up to my window. "Come here, let me show you something."

The snake is now stretched out all the way. "Look at him, he likes the heat coming out of the window," Angelita says as she reaches up with her right hand. "Caballo's just like that snake, big and scary-looking, but if you know how to handle him right . . ."

"What are you going to do?" I ask, as she grabs the snake behind the head and then pulls him off the screen.

The snake wriggles itself into a muscular S shape. "Relax," she hisses as the snake's tongue flickers close to her cheek. Angelita gently runs her left hand up and down its length until the snake hangs limp like a thick cord. Then she walks it toward the fence. Angelita smiles at the snake. "Harmless," she hisses again and then tosses it into the tall grass.

"Angelita! I could never do that."

"You could if you knew it was a milk snake. I looked him up in the book. They're not poisonous." She laughs. "Caballo is like that snake, big and scary-looking, but if you know how to handle him, he's harmless."

The moon is drifting over the wild place between the camp and the tomato fields. I can feel it tugging on a little thread of sadness that's been stuck in my throat for weeks.

Caballo is asleep and Angelita is walking a little ahead of me. They'll never see the tears.

DOLORES DEMOCRATIC

When I walk into the kitchen the next morning, Dolores is stirring a steaming pot with a spoon the size of a shovel.

"*Hola, Dolores,*" I say and look inside the pot. "*¿Que es?*"

"Grits, straight from the box," Dolores says as she ladles out a bowl of the yellow stuff and then drops a big chunk of butter on top. She pushes it in front of me. "My son liked his grits with plenty of butter. Never touched it until it was all melted," she says and hands me a spoon.

"You have a son?"

Dolores nods. "Yep." Then she goes back to stirring the bubbling goo.

As I wait for the butter to melt I take out the

handkerchief with the broken plate and set it on the table. I've been carrying it around in my pocket since Caballo took my things out of my suitcase. I'm afraid he'll figure out that it's really important to me and just like my drawing book, he'll take it away from me.

"Looks like you're going to need some glue for that," Dolores says and shuffles off to her locker. She comes back carrying a cigar box, a little metal glue can, and a screwdriver.

She hands me the can and the screwdriver. "This here's the glue for your plate. You're going to need the screwdriver to open the can."

Then she slides the cigar box in front of me. "That there are my son's drawing things. He used to draw all the time, too—regular artist, he was. But then he changed—got interested in other things." Dolores places the palm of her hand gently on the top, as if the thin wood still holds the warmth of her son.

"Where is he now?" I ask.

"When he got older I couldn't handle him; had to send him up north to live with his father." Dolores opens the box and her fingers drift over the colored chalks, crayons, and pencils. "I haven't seen him in years," she says and gently slides it back to me. "Take 'em. I seen you drawing in the dirt out by the garbage cans; you need them more 'n I do. I carried that box around with me for years. It's time to give it up!"

I inspect my new treasure. "Thank you, Dolores!"

"Don't mention it, Julian," she says and leans in close.

"I heard they sent your brothers away." Dolores rubs my head like my mother used to. "It just isn't fair. They should try and keep brothers together."

"It's Caballo," I mumble, as I sharpen a new yellow pencil.

Dolores wipes her hands on her apron and floats to the serving window. "That Caballo is a piece of work. Come over here, I want to show you something." She leads me to the little window where the dirty plates come in. "From here you can see things clear, like looking into one of them ant farms."

"What do you mean?"

Dolores leans in close again. "I've been reading the papers, and it seems to me that Caballo is just like the old dictator that flew away *and* the one who took over. Nobody voted them in and you can't vote them out. That's a dictator for you. But here in America we don't put up with no dictators. We elect them in and if we don't like them we elect 'em out and then we send them out to pasture. No ifs, ands, or buts!" She points at Caballo. "Look at him. He's a dictator all right."

Out in the dining hall, Caballo is sitting at the end of a long table right in front of the fan, shoveling large spoonfuls of grits into his mouth.

"Isn't that something? You've got the same thing here that you left back home! You can't get away from 'em."

"Can you do something about Caballo? Can you help us?" I ask.

"What am I going to do?" Dolores shrugs. "I'm just

the cook around here. I can't raise too much dust, I need the job!"

As Caballo is scraping up the last of his grits, a younger boy walks over and puts his dessert on Caballo's tray. The boy stands in front of the table waiting for Caballo to look up and put him on the right side of his friends and enemies mental list.

"You kids have to teach him a lesson, put him in his place," Dolores grumbles and heads back to the stove.

I pick up the screwdriver. "Put him in his place?" I think I might have a plan and it calls for a screwdriver.

"But you got to do it democratic, like we do it here," she says and lifts the hot pot off the stove.

Dolores walks up behind me, places her warm hand on my shoulder. "Butter's melted—eat your grits before they get cold."

I poke the yellow lake of butter into the grits and then taste it. I won't tell Dolores that it tastes like buttered cardboard. "What's democratic?" I ask.

"Democratic is when people get together, talk things over, and then decide what's best for all of them, and not for some big shot somewhere. It works because everybody's vote counts the same."

As Dolores bangs around the kitchen I push my grits around the plate and think about The Dolores Democratic Way. It sounds a lot more complicated than my plan.

Dolores thumps a large sack of powdered mashed potatoes up onto the table. When she stops to catch her breath she sees that I haven't touched my grits. She raises her sweaty eyebrow and gives me a look that I don't need to translate. I take a deep breath and shovel the grits into my bulging mouth as quick as I can swallow.

Just as I finish the last spoonful Dolores bangs a large pot up on the stove. I slip the screwdriver into my pocket, place the glue on top of the cigar box, and then jump off the stool.

If I don't carry out my plan now, I might lose my nerve.

"Thank you, Dolores!" I yell, and head for the door.

Dolores strikes a match and—*poof, whoosh*—the hissing gas lights up in a golden ring. "Hey, don't forget to return my glue and screwdriver when you finish!" she calls as she adjusts the yellow flame to blue on the tip.

PLANS AND TRAPS

Next morning after everyone has gone into the cafeteria for breakfast, I sneak over to Caballo's bottom bunk. The mattress of the top bunk rests on a net of springs and wires, attached to the metal frame by wire hoops. I wedge the screwdriver into a metal hoop, then pry it open just a little. I've got it all figured out. Every day I'll open a few hoops until big Ernesto on the top bunk comes crashing down on top of Caballo. That'll teach him a lesson.

I've opened only four hoops when the squeal of the door startles me. I frantically search for a place to hide the screwdriver. As I tuck it under the green blanket I see Angelita walking toward me.

"Where have you been?" I ask. "I was looking all over for you yesterday."

Angelita sits down at the end of the bunk, but she doesn't look at me. "They sent Pepe to a foster home."

"No!"

Angelita shrugs. "It's a nice family. I went to the house with Pepe yesterday. It's not too far away from here. I can go see him on the weekends. We got lucky."

"How come you didn't go with him?"

"They only had room for one kid. I'm going to miss him."

"I'm sorry, Angelita. I'm going to miss Pepe, too."

"He'll be fine. At least he's with a family and not in an orphanage or a group home." Angelita looks up at the underside of Caballo's bunk, then nods her head. "I get it. I know what you're doing," she says and points up at the loose metal loops. "I want to help."

"Angelita, are you sure? I thought you felt sorry for him."

"I did, but then I thought about what you said and decided you're right. We can't just let him get away with everything."

"Great," I say, happy to have a partner.

"Now, let's get to the cafeteria before Caballo misses us and comes looking for us. We'll meet after breakfast on top of the shed room."

After lunch, I climb up to the roof and wait for Angelita. When she finally pops her head over the edge she's got a little blue notebook with her. She sits down, takes out a short pencil, and opens the notebook. "Ok, shoot. Give me your ideas."

"I think we should start simple," I say as I pace along the edge of the roof. "Thumbtacks on his chair, tying his shoelaces together ... then we can put sugar under his pillow to give the ants something to snack on." Angelita is smiling as she hands me the notebook.

We keep switching back and forth, and the pranks get wilder and more elaborate until the notebook is half full. Then we stop to decide which ones we could actually do without getting caught.

Later on that day we were huddled at the end of picnic table going over our list when Marta walked by and asked what we were doing. When Angelita looked at me I could tell that she was dying tell her.

I nodded. "Go ahead."

At first Marta listened very seriously, then a little smile started to creep across her mouth. By the time we finished reading her our list she was laughing so hard that a big vein popped out on her forehead and wiggled like a little blue snake into her curly black hair. I don't think I had ever seen her laugh.

"Marta, would you like to help?" I asked. "But you have to swear that you won't tell anyone else."

Marta did promise not to tell but the next day Marta brought Ramón, a friend from Havana.

"Don't worry," Marta said very seriously. "We can trust Ramón."

Ramón is twig-thin and the fastest kid in the whole camp. Everyone calls him La Balla, the bullet. Yesterday he squeezed himself into Ernesto's locker and waited for him. When Ernesto opened the locker, Balla jumped out screaming. Ernesto fainted, and then got stuck under the bunk. A couple of the big kids chased Balla around the camp for hours. He would let them get fingertip close and then he'd streak off. Finally he got bored with the chase and just disappeared. He must have crawled into an air vent, or a clothes hamper, because no one saw him again until he showed up here today with Marta.

Even after we made him swear not to tell anyone what we were doing, he brought in two brothers who had just arrived, José and Gustavo. Their father was a chemist in Havana. They say that they can make anything we want to pop, fizz, stick, or smell bad from stuff everybody has under the kitchen sink. After José and Gustavo joined us, Marta announced, "That's it. No more new kids. It's already hard to meet without Caballo getting suspicious."

We meet every morning after breakfast on top of the shed to talk and to decide on the trick for that day. There is no boss or dictator in our group. That means that we listen to everybody's ideas and then vote on the ones we like.

We're trying to do things democratic like Dolores says it's done in America.

José and Angelita even wrote something they call a *constitution*. Angelita reads it at the beginning of every meeting. It ends with ". . . and most important, our mission is to get rid of El Caballo, the dictator, or make his life as miserable as possible." She says a lot of other things but that's the only part I listen to.

Every day we set a new trap and then wait for Caballo to fall for it. Every day more kids come to watch him pick ants out of his hair, or roll around on the floor moaning and scratching. With each new trick they linger a little longer and laugh a little louder. Every day they are less afraid that Caballo might see them. But I'm still too scared to look Caballo in the eye and tell him what I think of him.

Now that there is something to talk about and look forward to each day, the kids are much happier. Caballo, unfortunately, is not getting any smaller, but he is getting meaner.

This morning Marta suggests that we find another way to deal with Caballo. "We are making his life miserable, but he is making our lives miserable, too. Mark my words, the kids who are laughing now will be complaining soon. It might be fun, but it is not effective. We have to find a more intelligent and civilized way to deal with him."

Gustavo insists that we've gotten too good to quit, while José points out that it would be almost impossible to find anything else we could do that is as much fun. I agree with Gustavo and José but I think Marta's way is the smartest. The discussions keep going round and round until we see kids gathering by home plate for the morning game.

"Time for a compromise!" Marta announces. "We'll do one more trick while we are studying the problem." Then she stands up with a sly smile on her face. "And I have the perfect plan for our last surprise."

When Marta takes off her oversized glasses, her eyes look like little raisins. "My plan is based on two simple observations I have made about Caballo. Number one, he changes into his good pants right before dinner. Number two, he washes those pants once a week—always on Tuesday—the same day I work in the laundry." We watched her carefully put on her glasses, blinking each eye, making sure the lenses were spotless. Then she described her plan step by step, making it perfectly clear like her glasses.

"For the last step"—she waves a small silver tool, forked like the tip of a snake's tongue, and smiles—"my seam splitter. And I will do the rest."

THE REVOLUTION

It's dinnertime and I'm standing at the end of the table behind a pond of thick brown gravy, spoon in hand. I can see Gustavo sitting at the first table folding and unfolding a ten-dollar bill. La Balla, wearing a red handkerchief, cowboy style, is fidgeting next to him. I spot Caballo at the door and lift my spoon. La Balla pulls the handkerchief over his face and slips under the table.

Caballo cuts to the head of the line. He slides his tray along, stacking and piling on more food than any two people could eat. When he gets to me his eyes are glued to the greasy brown lake in front of me.

"Load on the gravy!" he growls without even looking up.

Gustavo winks at me as I flood Caballo's plate with the

greasy brown stuff. When Caballo slides his tray off the table, Gustavo steps up and "accidentally" drops the ten-dollar bill right in front of him. Caballo sees the bill. When he bends over to pick it up, a loud ripping noise cuts shreds through the room. The dining hall is quiet and everyone's eyes are on Caballo as he straightens up. He reaches for the split middle seam in the back of his pants. He must be feeling a breeze in the wrong place. Then La Balla, with his handkerchief covering his face, Old West bank robber style, flashes by and snatches Caballo's dessert right off his tray. Caballo lunges for him but stops when he hears the ripping noise again. Gustavo leisurely strolls to the big fan and then turns it on.

Caballo is standing still as a statue under the American and Cuban flags. The flags and the four loose pieces of fabric hanging off his belt are now snapping and waving in the electric breeze. We all stand up and start singing the Cuban national anthem.

Caballo, confused, half turns toward the flags but when he turns back, string beans, chocolate cake, and slippery mashed potatoes start raining down on him. This was not part of our plan but we join in throwing food and knocking over chairs. We sing the national anthem and the polka-dot bikini song at the same time. Caballo looks around at the wild crowd and then ducks out the back door.

Every bit of fear, anger, and sadness we've been carrying around, the frustration that drove us around the base-ball field, the uncertainty we wove into an endless variety of hats, has been cut loose with only one purpose: to turn this cafeteria into a slippery zoo.

Angelita and I are dancing on a groaning table like its New Year's Eve, as if our revolution is over and Caballo the dictator has grabbed all the desserts and flown away. Now I understand why those people in Havana were throwing chairs through the windows and ripping parking meters out of the ground with their bare hands.

When Caballo finally comes back with the director, they just stand in the back of the room with their arms crossed. The director isn't yelling or commanding us to stop. I guess he's just letting our springs unwind.

It doesn't take long before we are too tired to shout, climb, or sing anymore. Almost all at once and without a word from the director we sit down on the sticky benches and wait for him to walk up to the front of the room.

In a calm, even tone the director reminds us that we are here as guests and that destroying the things that were given to us out of charity and goodwill makes us look like ungrateful, wild animals.

As he speaks many hang their heads, but Marta does not. She stands up and in a calm voice says, "We are not ungrateful, wild animals, and if you don't listen to our complaints about Caballo, this will not be the last time this happens."

The director looks surprised. "Are you threatening me, young lady?"

Marta stares back at him unfazed.

"There will be no English lessons," he announces. "No trip to Miami, no breakfast, lunch, or dinner until everything is cleaned up. Romeo!" he yells. Caballo and his gang come back carrying brooms, mops, and buckets. They made us sweep, wash, and polish all day until the cafeteria was actually cleaner than it had ever been. Right before dinner we were sent out with bologna sandwiches while Caballo and his friends sat down to a hot meal in the clean cafeteria.

CABALLO ROJO

After our cafeteria revolution, Caballo watched us like a hawk. If he saw more than two people talking he or one of his helpers would swagger over and break up the discussions. We had to pass notes at the baseball games and communicate with hand signals.

While Marta and Angelita tried to think up a more civilized way of getting rid of Caballo, José and Gustavo were busy gathering things from the kitchen and the cleaning closets. They would disappear for hours and wouldn't tell me what they were doing.

"Marta is not going to like this," I said, when they laid out their plan and asked me to help.

"Neither is Caballo." Gustavo smiled, his face glowing with pride and anticipation.

Today is the first Sunday of the month and everyone is in bathing suits waiting for the station wagon that brings the new arrivals. Lately, Caballo has been welcoming all newcomers with a personal dunking to make sure they know he is the boss.

When I see the station wagon turn into the camp, I signal by lifting my hat and running my hand through my hair. Gustavo and José are standing by the side door to the kitchen. Gustavo lifts his hat and then they disappear inside. The station wagon drives into the yard and we all rush out to greet the new kids. I make sure to reach the doors first. Instead of yanking them open, I lean into them and cover the handles, stalling so that when Caballo gets there, Gustavo and José are right behind him.

Caballo pulls one of the two newcomers out. We crowd around, pushing real close as he hustles his victim to the pool. With the light touch of experienced pickpockets, Gustavo and José stuff Caballo and the newcomer's pockets with the frozen packets of a powerful red dye that Gustavo made.

Caballo pushes the new kid in and then jumps in after him but no one else joins them. We all stand around the pool as Caballo dunks his hapless victim, and we watch for signs that the dye packets are melting.

At first it's just delicate tendrils radiating red out of their pockets, but then as Caballo thrashes about, long red fingers dissolve into rich crimson veils, and then turn into a billowing, dangerous-looking cloud.

Spellbound, like spectators at a fireworks display, we shout and point at the vivid, unexpected color. When Caballo sees the red skirt of dye billowing around him he leaps out of the pool, his hair, skin, bathing suit, even his toes are all red. We're laughing as he points at us and orders his friends to grab us, but they're all laughing too. Caballo chases us, but we scatter in every direction. Gustavo smiles at the edge of the crowd because the longer Caballo waits to wash the dye off the longer it will stay on his skin.

The next day Caballo is wearing a long shirt and pants when he comes out to make his announcement. He holds up a piece of paper and reads, "No one will be allowed in the pool until the guilty ones come forward and confess!"

Gustavo and I ducked into the back of the crowd as he finished. Gustavo nodded proudly at Caballo, whose hair, neck, wrists, and hands were still bright red. Gustavo whispered in my ear, "That dye has staying power."

THE DEMOCRATIC WAY

Now that we can't swim, we're doomed to roast in the sun. For the last four days, a hot and gloomy crowd has been gathering after lunch to watch Caballo splash alone in the cool waters of the pool. There are no trees for shade, and it's as hot as an oven inside the metal buildings. More than once I've heard kids grumbling that the culprits who dyed Caballo should turn themselves in for the good of all. They never complained before, but this time Caballo took away the one privilege that we could not live without.

Angelita and I were helping Dolores in the kitchen when she pulled us aside and said, "All them tricks you been pulling on Caballo, they're not working. He's still here, and meaner than ever. I hear you can't use the pool now. If it was me, I'd try something else!"

"What else can we do, Dolores?" Angelita asked.

"First off, by now you should know that you don't fight fire with fire; you fight fire with water," Dolores declared.

"What do you mean?"

Dolores leaned in close and whispered, "Look, I can't be starting no trouble here, but I will tell you this, you're going about it the wrong way. You've got to do it democratic, like we do it here, not like they did it back home. Think about it: what did you get for all that fighting and revolution?"

"A dictator," Angelita said.

"You got to get everybody together, write petitions, call your congressman! And then vote that scoundrel out! Do it democratic."

"What's a petition?" I asked.

"I don't think we have a congressman," Angelita said.

"You don't know what a petition is?" Dolores shook her head and then looked up at the clock. "No time to explain now; I've got to get my shopping list for next week's meals to the director before he leaves," she said as she tore off her apron. "Go to the library!"

Dolores was heading out the door when Angelita asked, "Are you going to help us?"

Dolores shook her head. "No. I need this job. If they find out I'm putting ideas in your heads, it's good-bye, Dolores."

"Is that democratic?" Angelita asked sarcastically.

Dolores looked at Angelita as she pushed open the screen door. "It's like I said, Angelita, I need this job." Then she slammed the door shut.

"Let's go ask Marta," I said. "She's always reading—she knows everything."

Marta listened closely while we told her exactly what Dolores had said. When we finished, her fingers went back to weaving the palm fronds into her new hat creation: a broad-brimmed campesino hat with a swan on top.

Finally, Marta put down the hat. "Dolores is right," she said. "It's not working. We've been doing things the old way, the way we learned it. But he's better at it than we are. We have to learn a new way, the democratic way. That's what we've been looking for." Marta stood up and paced back and forth behind the bench.

"There are more of us than there are of them. We have to organize everybody, write a petition, and get signatures. We'll find people outside the camp that will listen to us; if they can't help us then maybe they'll know someone else who can."

"Who's got a pencil?" Marta asked as she dug a piece of paper out of her pocket.

"I do," I said.

Marta slid the paper over. "Now we can make a plan!"

We made a list of all the things that had to be done, put them in order, and put our initials next to the jobs we thought we could do best. We showed the list to José,

Ramón, and Gustavo so that they could pick their jobs. Finally we talked about what a petition is and what we wanted it to say.

Marta warned us that until we were ready to start, we had to keep our plans a secret.

"I'm sure that Caballo will find out eventually, but we need time to get the names and then make the calls. If we try to make all these calls from the phone in the director's office, Caballo will find out what we are up to and put a stop to it right away. We'll use the pay phone outside the dormitory," she said.

When everything was ready, Angelita and Marta started collecting signatures for the petitions and telephone numbers, while Ramón and José collected the dimes and nickels we would need for the pay phone. My job was to make little drawings to give to the kids who donated money.

RED X

Angelita has been bringing me the paper, mostly airmail stationary, thin as onion skin. I fold it in four and then, using the edge of the picnic table to get it straight, rip it along the folds.

I reach for the small stack of the almost-square blank pieces by my left hand and draw the first thing that comes to mind: Marta's hats, airplanes, the camp station wagon, Caballo with a beard and cigar in his mouth. When I finish a drawing I place it in the pile by my right hand, then reach for another piece of paper.

I'm on my last piece of paper when Angelita bursts out of the dormitory.

She's walking really fast toward the picnic table, looking back at the door every other step.

"Put them away," she says and then points at my drawings. "Caballo is coming and he's *mad*."

That's all I need to hear. I collect all my drawings and then slide them under my legs.

I can hear Caballo's footsteps as I start a sun and lollipop tree drawing like I used to do when I was a little kid. Caballo's shadow falls across my smiling sun and then his big hand lands on my box of pastels. They're very soft. If he presses any harder on them they'll turn to dust.

"You think you're so smart—you and your little friends." He breathes into my face. His skin is blotchy red, the dye is starting to wear off.

I had never looked at Caballo this closely before. The egg we had for breakfast is still wedged in between his teeth and gums, and I never noticed how the little hairs growing in the space between his eyes are trying to make two eyebrows into one.

"I know everything that goes on here!" Caballo says, pointing a pastel green finger back at the camp. He flicks a drop of sweat from the tip of his red nose and leaves a green smudge in between his nostrils. Ever since the pool trick he's been real jumpy and nervous. He looks as if he's been sleeping with one eye open, probably waiting for the next surprise. I almost feel sorry for him, because of what

Angelita told me about bullies. He can't help himself. He's carrying a heavy bag that he can't put down.

He drops a piece of paper on top of my drawing. It's the front page of the petition and the very first name, the first signature, is mine.

"I've known all along. I've been watching you, waiting for the right moment."

"Where did you get that?" I ask, trying to control my trembling voice.

"I have friends everywhere!" Caballo boasts. "Friends who want to help me, not people like you who sneak around behind my back!"

I can't look up at him so I stare at my hands.

"You better start packing. The car will be here tomorrow afternoon to take you and two other kids to the airport."

When I don't look up, Caballo asks, "Don't you want to know where you're going?"

When I don't answer, he picks up my box of pencils and chalks. He turns it over in his hands.

"I see you carrying these around with you everywhere you go."

He wants me to beg him to put them down. When I don't say anything, he drops the box on the ground. As I reach for it, he steps on it. I hear the chalk crunching under his heel.

I want to yell and kick him as hard as I can, but I can't because that's what he wants me to do. He wants me to get mad and do something, so that then he can squash me like a bug. But the real reason I'm not moving is that he's still too big, and I'm still too scared.

My hand is trembling as I grab my one remaining pastel. He's standing over me, his big fists ready at his sides. I start drawing again and it seems like an eternity before he turns and then walks away. When he's out of sight I get down on my knees and sort through the crushed box. Most of the pastels have turned to dust and almost every pencil has been splintered. I get up and kick the box away. I'm as mad at myself as I am at Caballo. I'm such a coward.

Angelita puts her arm over my shoulder. "I'm sorry about your box, Julian. He shouldn't have done that."

"It's my fault," I huff. "I shouldn't have let him ever see it. He knows he can do anything he wants to me and nothing will happen to him!"

"Don't be mad at yourself. I'll find out who's leaving with you, and then we'll know where you're going," Angelita says.

"Don't bother, Angelita. It doesn't matter. I'm not old enough to go to the orphanage where they sent my brothers." I ground my last crayon into the paper. "All the kids my age are going to the other place. I'm not going there." One of the boys that was sent there had written a letter that was passed around. We all read it. He had gone over the last line so many times with his ballpoint pen that he had worn through the paper. "No matter what, don't let them send you here!" It said.

90 Miles to Havana

"You have to go," Angelita says. "They'll make you."

"I don't have to go anywhere I don't want to!" I say as loud as I can, not caring who hears me. The instant those words came out of my mouth I felt a little better. "Didn't Marta tell us that when she got here, there was a kid who took off every time the car came to take him to the airport?"

"I remember," Angelita says, "and when the car left, he came back. He did that a few times, but they did finally send him away!"

A plan begins spinning in my head. It's amazing how clear things look when you have no choice, when there's no question that you have to jump, do something.

"Tomorrow is Saturday; the station wagon's coming in the morning to take Caballo's friends to Miami. Then it will come back for me and the two other kids in the afternoon, right?"

"So?" Angelita asks.

"So we have to disappear before the station wagon comes back in the afternoon."

"Just how are you going to make yourself disappear?"

"We'll get on the morning trip to Miami, that's all," I say as if I know exactly what I'm going to do. I don't know why but I feel strangely confident. I might not be as brave and tough as Gordo or smart and strong like Alquilino but I can invent—make things up as I go along—better than both of them put together. Bebo said so.

Angelita is looking at me like I've lost my mind. "Julian, Caballo is in charge of making up that list—you're not going to be on it. Where would you go anyway? You can't just wander around the streets!"

"Don't worry, I have a plan for getting on the list. And we can go to Tomás boat. He wants us to come; he said he could use my help with his boat engine. You still have the map, right?"

"What do you mean, *we*?" Angelita asks.

"I thought, since Pepe is gone, you could come with me."

"I can't just run away!"

"Why not?"

"I told you already, Julian. The family that took Pepe said they might take me, too."

"What if they don't? What if they send you away first? Besides, we can always come back!" Then, before she could complain, I started on the list of things that we'll need. "And don't forget the map to Tomás's boat.

"Julian, this is crazy. I don't think you can do it."

"Angelita, I have to do it!"

THE LAST HOOP

This morning questions and doubts are buzzing around my head like hungry mosquitoes. What will Caballo do to me if he catches me? What if Angelita doesn't come with me? I feel lonely and scared just thinking about leaving. What if I get lost? Maybe this is a crazy idea. But then one little thought lights up the dark edges of the others: this might be a crazy idea, but it's my idea. My brothers are not here to tell me I can't do it or that I should do it some other way.

The alarm clock goes off. It's time to go. I land soft as a feather and then reach under the bottom bunk. The bag Angelita packed for me is right where it should be. Inside I find the two short lengths of chain, two combination locks, and the screwdriver. I can still back out if I have to but Angelita is probably up already. I push the screen open, and then shove my suitcase out the window.

I sneak up to Caballo, snoring in his bottom bunk. His feet are poking through the metal brackets at the end of his bed and he looks even bigger lying down. I put the bag under his bed and check my watch again: thirty seconds to go. My hands are shaking as I take out the screwdriver. Leaning over Caballo, I carefully open up eight more of the rings that hold up the top bunk. Now there are only four thin loops of metal left, one in the middle of each side— surely not enough to hold up the hefty Ernesto mumbling in his sleep above Caballo.

There's still time to crawl back into bed—forget the whole thing. No one has seen me yet and the metal rings are still holding.

When Ernesto's alarm goes off, it startles me and I drop my screwdriver. I dive and catch it before it hits the ground. Then I roll under Caballo's bunk as the lump above me starts to move.

Caballo yells, "Ernesto, time to get up!"

Ernesto's not moving; he must be deep in a dream. The metal frame shakes when Caballo kicks the underside of his bunk. Ernesto whimpers.

Caballo kicks him harder.

Then I hear the screech of metal grating on metal followed by a titanic thump as Ernesto and his bed crash down on top of Caballo.

Caballo screams, "Ma—Ma," and I'm almost crushed by the falling mattress.

My arms are pinned to my side and I can't reach the chains. I didn't think of this, but I can't give up now. I squirm and manage to free my hands.

I wrap the chain around the frames of Ernesto and Caballo's bunk and pull it to the other side and padlock it. Then I have to squeeze and twist myself around to reach the bottom of the frame to padlock that end. When I finish Caballo is trapped in a metal cage made of the frames chained together. I can feel him struggling above me and yelling for Ernesto to get off.

A laughing, jeering crowd is gathering around him as I crawl out from under his bunk and start to walk away. I know I should just slip away but I can't resist. I walk back, lean over Caballo, and look him in the eyes.

"Now we're even!"

Caballo stops thrashing around. He's lying perfectly still as I run to the door. "Stop him!" he bellows.

Before I step outside, I grab the hanging clipboard with his list.

The driver is trying to see what's going on inside the dormitory, so he doesn't see me adding my name to the list. As Angelita walks by with my suitcase, I add her name to the list as well. Then I run to the doorway to hurry the other kids into the car.

"Caballo is kind of tied up right now," I say to the driver, waving the clipboard at him.

"What's all the fuss about?" he asks.

"Someone fell out of their bunk, that's all," I say and then push the clipboard in front of his face. "Here's the list; we're all here."

The driver is slowly pronouncing each syllable as he reads the first name on the list. I have to do something or we're not going to make it. I stand on my tiptoes and read the rest of the names out as Angelita pushes the kids into the car.

"Looks like we have a full load today," I say.

The driver looks a little annoyed, so I smile up at him. "Just trying to be helpful. Don't you have another run to the airport right after this one? That's a lot of driving to do!"

The driver checks his watch. "*Sí,* we better get going."

ALONE IN MIAMI

"So those big *Americanos* stuck him in a dryer." The driver chuckles. "They kept pumping in dimes, just to watch him tumble around." All the way into the city he's been telling stories about the children who were not careful on their visit to Miami.

As he parks the car the driver raises one bushy eyebrow. "Remember stay together...and stay away from the Laundromats. Some gringos have a strange sense of humor." He laughs.

Angelita and I are standing at the back of the group in front of a Cuban coffee shop the size of a walk-in closet. The smell of the coffee is making me homesick.

"I want everybody back by four, *me entienden?*" the driver yells, and then downs a thimble-sized paper cup of black coffee.

As the group starts to drift away, I snatch my suitcase out of the back and we hurry off in the opposite direction.

"I think he was trying to scare us, don't you?" I ask Angelita.

"I believe him," she answers and takes a piece of paper out of her back pocket.

"What's that?" I ask, as she carefully unfolds the paper.

"The map," she says and runs her finger over the blue line that ends in an *X* on a river next to a highway. She looks around and then without hesitation points down the street. "This way," she says and then folds up the map.

As we walk, Angelita repeats the name of each street over and over.

"Angelita, what are you doing?"

"Memorizing the names so we don't get lost."

We walk into a busy street crowded with men in suits rushing from one building to the other. In a department-store window a family of naked mannequins waits for someone to come and dress them. Tourists in flowered shirts sift through a parade of colorful bicycles spilling out of a shop onto the sidewalk. We linger for a moment, savoring the smell of new paint and running our fingers through the soft foxtails hanging from the handlebars.

Construction workers in yellow helmets swarm in and

out of a building wheezing clouds of white dust. A crane dances a metal beam to three men, high up in the rising steel frame. They grab the swinging beam, nudge it into place, and then bolt it onto the Tinkertoy frame. If I listen and look just right, the growl of engines, beeping of the horns, and the tack-tack of a jackhammer turn into music, then the men in their yellow hats almost look like they're dancing to the beat of the song. But the music here is louder, harsher than the music of Havana. There you could hear conversations breathing out of cool entryways, caged birds singing on a balcony, and the muffled *clack-clack* of someone mopping the floor inside. Here there are no voices or songbirds, just the crunch and grind of machines.

We've been walking for hours, and Angelita is still reading the street signs. Every block, every name she calls out, takes me farther away from the camp. Not just the kids, the bunk beds, and the metal buildings, but everything that was connected to it, like my brothers, parents, and my home. Every other block I think about what would happen if I went back, but then I remember Caballo's face pressed between the bedsprings, his angry eyes. I'm scared and excited at the same time.

Angelita checks her map and then announces, "Pirate Angel's!" She points at the sign blinking red in broad daylight. "This must be where Tomás gets his free sugar," she says.

"The pirate girl on the sign looks just like you," I say earnestly.

Angelita punches me on the arm. "Does not! She's a lot older." We walk in and climb up on two red stools. Angelita takes off her cap. "That feels much better," she says, and shakes out her shiny black hair.

A waitress in a red headscarf and white pirate's blouse puts a place mat down in front of us and pulls a pencil and pad from her belt where her pirate's sword would be. "What'll you have?" We order two Pirate Pepsis and study the place mat decorated with a map of Miami. The red pirate's script reads, Pirate Angel's Miami. Angelita points at a spot on a ribbon of blue running through the city.

"Tomás lives around here," she says and then takes out her own map. It's the same place mat but this one has notes scribbled all over it.

"Here you go, tall and cool," the waitress says and places our drinks in front of us. "What do you have there, a treasure map?" She leans in close. "Hey that looks like Tomás's handwriting. I'd recognize it anywhere."

"Tomás?" Angelita asks.

"Tomás? *Sí.*" The waitress turns toward the kitchen. "Doctor, come on out here," she yells. "We got two patients for you!"

A silver-haired man in a dirty white uniform gently shoulders the door open. He wipes his hand and then extends it toward Angelita.

"Alejandro De La Vega, at your service."

"I'm Angelita, and this is Julian."

"Where are you from?"

"Havana."

"I'm from Havana, too." The gentleman glances back toward the kitchen. "A surgeon there, dishwasher here." The doctor looks down at his pruny hands. "It seems like a million years ago.... I am sorry, did I hear you say that you are looking for Tomás?"

"He gave me this map," Angelita says. "He said we could visit him anytime."

"You're coming from the camp?"

"Yes," I answer.

"Tomás has told me a great deal about that camp. He used to go there in the beginning to help get it ready for the Pedro Pan kids. He's always talking about the cook, Doris?"

"Dolores." Angelita laughs.

"Yes, Dolores, excuse me. Tomás says that the camp is full of kids that came here all alone. Did you come without your parents?"

We both nod.

"It must be hard for you," the doctor says shaking his head slowly, "and a nightmare for your parents."

"Doctor!" A booming voice from the kitchen rattles the silverware. "I'm not paying you to talk to the customers. Remember, dishwashers are a dime a dozen."

The doctor waves at the kitchen door. "He won't fire me, doctors who wash dishes are not a dime a dozen."

Why are you washing dishes?" I ask.

"Because I have three children, and they need a place to live and food to eat."

"You came with your children?" I ask.

"We left earlier when it was easier to get out."

"Can't you find a job as a doctor?" Angelita asks.

"To be a doctor here you have to pass the tests. The Cuban license is no good here."

"You mean you have to go back to school?"

"Yes, I go at night and wash dishes all day, but you know, I'm happy to be here and lucky to have a job and my children. All the trouble and hardships we've had to face here are nothing compared to the heartbreak of parents sending their children away." The doctor stands up, winks at the waitress, and puts two egg salad sandwiches and a handful of sugar packets in a brown paper bag. "Tomás lives down this road a bit, after the little cement bridge. Look for the trail down to the river." The doctor slips the bag to Angelita, then looks at his watch. "The last bus back downtown is at three-thirty."

"Then we better hurry," Angelita says and swings off the stool. As we head out the door the doctor waves. "Say hello to Señor Tomás!"

Angelita and I walk down a treeless avenue. There are sandy open spaces on either side waiting for new buildings, and then an occasional used car lot with rows of like-new cars waiting to be sold.

"This must be the bus stop," Angelita says, pointing to a bench. We sit down and she hands me her map.

"You aren't coming, are you?" I ask.

"I already told you, Julian, I can't. There is still a chance Pepe's foster family might take me."

The sad feelings that I've been pushing down for so long are starting to bubble up again. They've been there for so long, but they're like splinters that are too deep to pull out; the only thing you can do is to ignore them. I grab my suitcase and start walking away.

"Julian!" Angelita yells. "Is that it? You just get up and leave like it doesn't matter to you?"

"Angelita, it does matter. What do you want me to do?" I mumble, feeling like my face is about to crack. "You know I can't go back there." Angelita gets up and stands in front of me. I know she wants a better answer.

"When Alquilino and Gordo got sent away, I had to learn how not to think about them, just like I learned how not to think about my parents. I guess by now I'm getting better at it." It's not really true, but I swallow hard and start walking away. The bus is rushing up the street toward us. When I hear the hiss of its doors opening I stop. "Good-bye, Angelita."

"I'm sorry I can't go with you, Julian."

Afraid that my legs are going to rebel and run back to the bus, I turn away as fast as I can.

"Remember, look for the path just past the bridge," Angelita yells out the window. "Tomás said that you can't miss it. I'll try to come back next weekend, I promise. *¡Cuidate*, Julian!"

I start walking away, listening to the grind of the bus getting softer.

"Caballo will never let her out again." The dark windows of an empty factory are looking down at me. They seem to be asking, "Why are you here; why all alone?"

I know if I don't keep walking fast, I'll change my mind and turn back. I try to remember how good I felt when I thought up this crazy plan. It might be a crazy plan, but it is *my* plan. Besides, it's too late to turn back. I already missed the last bus.

"I have to find Tomás."

When I see the bridge up ahead. I start feeling a little better.

But then I spot five guys leaning on a parked car just to the right of the bridge. They look like the kind of guys that could put someone like me in a dryer.

As I walk by, one of them points his cigarette at me. "Hey, where you going?"

I make believe I didn't hear him and keep walking.

A short guy with slick dark hair points at my suitcase. "Running away from home?" he says, and the others laugh.

I pull my suitcase close to my chest and walk faster.

"Hey, amigo!" he calls out.

I hear the car engine roar, and I start running. The car glides up behind me and someone yells, "Hey, amigo, there's no need to be rude!"

The car stops in the middle of the bridge, and the guys get out. Surrounded, I lean back against the railing.

I'm trying to stay calm, think my way out, make the

right choice: a long drop into muddy water, or a trip to the Laundromat and a long ride inside a dryer. They're getting closer. I balance my suitcase on the railing. Then I climb up next to it but my knee knocks into the suitcase.

"No!" I scream as I watch it dropping, getting smaller and then splashing into the muddy water.

"What are you doing? Don't jump, we're not going to hurt you!" one of the guys yells.

I'm watching my suitcase with all my clothes, my notebook, all the addresses I'll need, spinning away in the brown water. Then I remember the gold bird. My mother is going to kill me if I loose it!

I balance on the thin rail. This is higher than the high board at the beach, and I was waiting until next year to try that.

"Don't jump!" the short guy says, as my suitcase spins downstream. I can't let it get away but my feet feel like they're glued to the railing—I can't make myself jump into the river or back on the sidewalk! I'm stuck and they're getting closer.

Then someone yanks on my belt, and I tumble back onto the sidewalk. They've got me; next stop, the Laundromat. I can't believe my eyes; Angelita is hovering over me like an angel.

"You're here?"

"Get up, stupid! Follow me!" She yanks on my collar,

then pulls me to the other side of the bridge, and disappears down the path. I trip and then slide down the steep muddy bank into the water. Angelita is already clinging to the floating suitcase when I swim up.

"I leave you for five minutes, and you get yourself into trouble," Angelita says as she tries to catch her breath.

The guys up on the bridge are laughing and pointing at me. "Hey, *Cubanito*, you're crazy, man!"

"What was that all about?" Angelita asks.

"I thought they were going to take me to the Laundromat, put me in the dryer. The driver said gringos have a strange sense of humor!"

"We weren't going to hurt you!" one of the guys yells. "Crazy Cubans!"

Angelita is looking at me when I finally figure out that maybe they didn't mean any harm. "What am I going to do with you, Julian?" she says and pats my arm. "Don't worry about it. It could happen to anybody."

"I always thought you'd be coming with me," I say.

"Don't get your hopes up," she says, as we twirl downstream in the warm tide.

"I'm glad you're here," I say as the sounds of flowing water and birdcalls mix with the soft hum of the highway above us. The tall trees growing on the steep banks block out most of the sunny bustle of the city.

Wrecked cars and piles of old tires peek out from under the green blanket of vines and bushes creeping up the banks. Sleepy turtles roll off their logs as we sweep around a bend. Then Angelita points at an old wooden boat ten feet up the bank.

"That must be Tomás's boat."

The boat is perched on tree trunks and an old refrigerator. A rope as thick as my wrist is wrapped around the hull and then tied off to a lemon tree. We paddle to a rough dock made of telephone poles and crates tied together.

Angelita calls out, "Tomás!" There's no answer, so we climb up a rickety ladder to the deck.

The tipped wooden deck is crowded with rusting engine parts, bent nails, bolts, and tin cans; orphaned stuff that Tomás has adopted. I walk over to a pile of tin cans, with a stack of flattened tin sheets next to it.

"That Tomás doesn't waste a thing," I say as I study the soup cans that have been cut and then hammered flat. Two buckets of rusty nails stand side by side; one is filled with crooked ones, in the other the straightened ones.

"I bet Tomás is a lot like Bebo," I say to Angelita as she steps over a ball of used tinfoil the size of a basketball.

"You never told me Bebo was a pack rat," Angelita says.

"Bebo doesn't have as much, but he uses whatever he's got lying around to make and fix things just like Tomás."

As we're talking, a boat chugs around the bend. The outboard motor sounds like an angry mosquito as it strains against the current. Tomás is standing on a pile of wooden planks in the middle of the overloaded boat. There is a man sitting in the back steering the boat across the current into the dock.

"I can't believe my eyes!" Tomás yells. "Angelita, Julian?" Tomás seems really happy to see us. "How are things at the camp?" he asks.

"Oh you know, the same I guess," Angelita says.

"Well, you're here, and that tells me something."

The guy in the back of the boat stands up and picks up a plank. "Hey, Tomás, the tide is changing," he says in English, but with a different accent than Dolores. "If we don't get unloaded soon I'll never get out of here and then you'll be making me dinner."

"*Jes, jes,*" Tomás says in his accented English, and waves at us. "Julian, Angelita, this is Dog. He's helping me with the boat."

We wave hello, and Dog tips an imaginary cap at us. "That's short for Sea Dog," he says and smiles at us.

"He's right about the tide," Tomás says as he grabs a plank. "I hate to put you to work. We'll catch up over dinner."

We help carry the heavy planks up the steep muddy bank as the Dog fiddles with the motor. It's not easy work, but we don't complain. As we take the last plank off the boat, Dog puts the engine in reverse and smiles. With his long sharp canines showing, Dog looks more like a wolf than a dog. He waves good-bye and speeds back toward the bend.

When we finish stacking the planks we wash up in the river.

"Tomás, how did you get the boat up there?" I ask.

"That's the way I found her, a hurricane tore her off her mooring and then carried her in here."

"What about its owner?"

"Owner? I'm the owner now. Dog says if you find a boat adrift you can claim it. He called it Right of Salvage—finders keepers."

Tomás leads the way up the ladder then opens a hatch at the back end of the boat and points at what looks like a pile of rusty metal. "Look at that engine, have you ever seen anything as beautiful?"

"That's incredible," Angelita says sarcastically. "Did it come with the seaweed?"

"It looks kind of rusty," I say.

"When I get through with that engine it will purr like a kitten," he says. Then we follow him down into a surprisingly clean, uncluttered cabin. We sit at a table neatly stacked with navigational charts. There is a shiny brass compass above us on a shelf, and blue life preservers hanging from pegs. "This is where I come to think my way around things. I've got to have order"—Tomás points at his head and laughs—"or this thing won't work!"

Then he holds up a small knife and an onion. "It's dinnertime. Who wants to help?"

I volunteer, and Tomás smiles as I cut the top and the bottom of the onion, peel back the skin, slice it in half, and then into quarters.

"I'll bet you worked in the kitchen with Dolores," he laughs.

"I watched Dolores peel hundreds of onions," I answer.

"You paid attention. I like that." Tomás scoops the onions into a dented frying pan and then lights a little brass stove. "So, what's your plan?"

"Plan?" I ask.

"I know you didn't come just to see the boat. You missed the last bus. What's going on at the camp?"

"Do you know Caballo?" I ask.

"Caballo? Sure. He's the reason I won't work at the camp. He's a crook. He wanted me to pay him for letting me work there. He said if I didn't, he'd find somebody else," Tomás shook his head. "I told him the reason we had a revolution back home was because of people like him. I never went back to the camp after that."

Now I like Tomás even better. I tell him about how Caballo sent my brothers away and how mean he's gotten. Tomás laughs when I tell him about all the tricks we played on him.

"It sounds like you got the revolution started! It's funny how these things follow us around."

"If I go back he'll make my life miserable first, and then they'll send me away to an orphanage or worse," I say.

"No, it would not be a good idea to go back," he says. "I don't blame you for running away, but still, it takes a lot of nerve to do what you did."

"I was more scared of what would happen if I stayed."

"I can understand that, I guess that's why I left, too."

He nods and looks around for an extra plate.

"Tomás, you never told me how you got out of Cuba," Angelita says.

"It was my father who got me out. He was afraid of what would happen to me if I stayed."

"Your father?"

"*Sí*, he was a mechanic in the navy. He hated it, but when I turned sixteen he insisted I join the navy and become a mechanic, too. I thought that was strange because he used to say that I could do much better than that.

"One day they sent us to Cárdenas Bay to fix a motor launch that belonged to his captain. We were on the dock when my father told me to row out and get started—he would join me later.

"When I got on board I saw that the gas tank was full, and that the waterproof compartment next to the wheel was crammed with charts for a trip—a trip to Florida.

"I started the engine and it was running like a top. I could tell right away that it had just been tuned—probably by him. Nobody can tune an engine like my father. He waved for me to run it, so I pulled up the anchor and flew across that bay. As I roared back past the dock I saw two naval officers standing with my father. The two navy guys were signaling for me to come in." Tomás smiled. "But my father was standing behind them, pointing north.

"That's when I figured out why he had talked me into

joining the navy, why he sent me out to tune an engine that he probably had just tuned. Just that like that"—Tomás snaps his fingers—"I decided. I pulled back on the throttle, and headed straight for the dock. At the last second I turned and sent up a rooster tail of water that soaked all three of them. I made one more pass laughing and hollering like a madman so that they wouldn't think that my father put me up to it. The last time I saw him he and the navy guys were yelling and shaking their fists at me, but then he stepped behind them and flashed me the good luck sign.

"I motored north thinking about how he must have planned the whole escape and never said a word to me—just in case. He did his part and now I have to do mine."

Angelita is standing next to the table clutching the plates to her chest, listening. "You left just like that? No clothes, no good-byes?"

"Not really. I found a change of clothes and some dollars in a locker below, but the thing that still really bothers me is that I didn't get to say good-bye to my mother."

"How could you just leave like that? That's something I'd have to think about for a while," she says as she lays out the three different-colored plates.

"I'm the same way, Angelita. I like to plan, get used to the idea. But there was no time for that. I had to decide on the spot; he made me jump." Tomás smiles. "I think my father knows me too well."

"Tomás, that took a lot more nerve than what I did. I had time to plan and decide," I say.

ARMANDO

This morning I find the forward cabin empty, the deck crowded with clucking seagulls, but no Angelita or Tomás.

Down in the galley, a cup of *café con leche* sits on the stove with a plate on top to keep it warm. The note sticking out from underneath the plate reads, *"Amigo, I'm off to the fields, El Toma-Tron calls me. Lazy Armando at the Fontainebleau Hotel always needs help. Catch the number 11 bus, just past the bridge. It will take you right to the hotel. Tell him Tomás sent you."* Below that, in a loopy, feminine script there's more: *Julian, you already know why I can't stay with you, but I had to make sure you got here safely. I'll stay in touch through Tomás. You're in good hands. Angelita.*

I knew that she had to go back, but still I was hoping.

"Shoo!" I yell and wave my arms as the flock of seagulls lifts off squawking and complaining. I'm alone on the bank of a strange river and I'm starting to get that scared, lonely feeling again.

I better get moving, do something, so that I won't think about Angelita or my brothers and my parents. Those thoughts only make me feel bad. I'm going to put on a clean T-shirt and get out of here.

When I open my suitcase, I see the blue lining and I think about my mother running her fingers along it. I'm trying to picture the little gold bird sleeping in there, and trying not to think about my mother's face.

Everything in the suitcase is wet, so I take out my shirts and pants and hang them around the cabin so they'll dry. I put on a clean shirt, wet and wrinkled, but clean, and head up the hill to the bus stop.

Sitting on the bus, I feel better. I have to pay attention; I don't want to miss the hotel. I wonder if Angelita got back to the camp. I miss her already.

When the bus driver announces, "Fontainebleau Hotel," I run out through the hissing door into a blue cloud of bus exhaust that's now drifting over the lush gardens of the hotel. As I walk past the tall metal gate, I notice that there is a guy guarding the front doors. The top hat and the circus general's uniform he's wearing makes him look important. He crosses his arms, steps in front of the door, and watches me walk around the fountain in the middle of the circular driveway.

Then he points at the gate, and yells, "Shoo!"

I stop in the middle of the driveway. "Shoo who?" I look behind me. "Shoo me?"

He points at me. "You, out!" he says in a tone of voice that a stray dog would understand. I plant my feet in the asphalt and cross my arms, too. Who does he think he is talking to me like that? My father used to take us to bigger and better hotels than this, and in Cuba the doormen didn't have to dress up like circus performers.

He starts walking in my direction and getting bigger with every step so I turn around and head for the gate.

As I walk out I look at my wet wrinkled shirt and grubby shorts. I guess I don't look like I belong here.

Just then, a yellow cab flies in through the gate and screeches around the other side of the fountain. I duck into the bushes as the doorman rushes over to open the door of the cab. He opens the trunk and sticks his head inside. As he struggles to pull out an enormous suitcase, I slip in through a smaller side door.

I make a beeline for the two brilliant stripes of blue sky and creamy, white sand glaring into the back of the dark lobby. I'm staring up at a chandelier the size of a car when someone grabs my shoulder.

"Excuse me, may I help you?" A little man wearing a red jacket and a Turkish hat with a gold tassel hanging in front of his stubby nose is standing behind me. He looks like an organ grinder's monkey. I wiggle free from the hairy paw gripping my shoulder.

"Are you a guest here?" the monkey man asks.

"Armando, I come to see Armando," I say.

"The guy with the umbrellas?" he asks.

"*Sí*, Armando."

He looks at me and curls his nostril as if I smell bad. "Follow me."

We cut across the lobby away from the beach, then into a big room full of black ladies in blue uniforms folding and then stacking sheets. The next room is full of men washing dishes; they're all speaking Spanish.

The monkey man grabs my arm and hustles me out of a side door. We rush past the garbage cans and then down a dirt path behind the swimming pool. The smell of suntan lotion and the sparkling blue water is making me home-sick. We walk around the pool to the edge of the sand and then he stops, wipes off his shiny little boots, and points at a striped tent down on the beach. I feel like asking him why we didn't just walk straight here, but I know the answer. He didn't want the guests to see me. I take my sneakers off and start walking across the hot sand to the tent.

When a sea breeze blows the tent flap open, I see a large man sitting back on a chaise lounge with what looks like a flock of yellow butterflies fluttering above his head. He's scribbling something into a yellow notebook.

"Armando?" I ask.

"Jes, un momento pliss," he says, not bothering to look up.

He tears out a yellow note, waves it at me, then hands me a safety pin.

"*Arriba*." He points over his head and to the right. As I pin up the piece of paper and say in Spanish, "I'm Julian, a friend of Tomás, the inventor of the Toma-Tron."

"Only English, *por favor*," he answers. "Speak English, I learn," he says and then points at the butterfly notes. "Facts are very important, Thomas Edison *invento el teléfono* by *accident.*"

Then he sits up and extends his hand in my direction. "*Un amigo de Tomás, el* Edison *Cubano,* is a friend of mine." Before we can shake, he waves his hand over his head with a flourish and then bows. "Armando in your service."

"Tomás said that you give me work." Armando motions for me to come closer; he reaches up and squeezes my arm. While holding my arm with one hand he opens his diction-ary with the other, and leafs to the right page. "Let's see, *fuerte, muy fuerte, sí,* estrong, very estrong," he says. His voice sounds very familiar to me.

Just then a woman, with dark glasses the size of saucers and shiny gold hair, pokes her head into the tent. "Armando dear, you promised to have our umbrella up before we came out." She walks right past me to Armando's side and puts her hand on his shoulder.

Armando stands up. "Mrs. Wilson, *mi amor,* I do not

forgotten." His voice is syrupy sweet as he ushers her out the door, "Ah jes, here it is"—he stops to read one of his notes—"In the shake of your lamb's tail, it will be did."

Mrs. Wilson giggles. "Oh, Armando!"

Armando gestures in my direction. "*Mi assistante* will bring to you."

"Hurry, Armando, my little Billy will be positively singed if we don't have an umbrella." Then she pushes the flap open. "*Pronto*, boy, *pronto!*" she says without even looking at me. Then she flashes Armando a red lipstick smile, and walks out into the sun.

"Julian! This first customer, Mrs. Wilson, is a good tipper! Sink it in deep, Julian—the wind is . . ." I wait as he looks up a word. "*Sí*, capricious. The wind is capricious today. *Capricious*—fickle, changeable."

I search in the pile for an umbrella, as Armando leafs madly through his dictionary. He's rolling a new word slowly in his mouth. I hear him read slowly, "*Singe*: to expose the carcass of a bird or animal to a flame in order to remove unwanted feathers, bristles, or hair!" Then he calls, "Julian, for Billy's sake, hurry!"

Billy's mother doesn't notice that the umbrella is much bigger than I am. She points the straw of her drink at her Billy. He looks up from his Tarzan comic as I try to push the umbrella into the sand. I want to tell him that I have the same comic book; it's back home under my bed, but he gives me a funny look and then rolls away. I don't like the way he looked at me. I get the feeling that he thinks he's better than me.

I manage to stand the umbrella up and pull it open just in time for a gust of wind to grab it. The umbrella leans dangerously in Billy's direction. The sand is flying as I wrestle the red monster upright. When I get it under control, I look at them and smile—both are wearing a layer of white sand stuck on the greasy suntan lotion. They're not happy.

Mrs. Wilson clutches her son and yells, "Ar-man-do!"

Armando stomps out and pushes the red umbrella deeper into the sand. He croons an apology and then bows to Mrs. Wilson and her itchy son. Suddenly I realize where I've heard that voice. "You're '*Amando Armando!*' Loving Armando. My mother listens to you every night." I stop and stare at him. He's a real famous person!

He pulls me back to the tent, gesturing theatrically. "My best tipper, and you almost kill her child!" he says, reverting to Spanish.

"Your mother *used* to listen me," he corrects, and bows his head. Then he straightens up and strikes a pose. "But mark my words, Armando will rise again!" Then he waves his dictionary at me. "First, I learn the English," he says as if he's narrating a movie about himself and his heroic quest. "In the meantime," he says in a normal tone of voice, "I'll set the umbrellas up in the morning, and you can take them down in the evening."

Armando disappears into the tent, and I'm left outside,

not sure what to do next. I'm still watching the tent flap waving in the breeze, when he pokes his head out.

"You are still here? How can I study with you standing there? Shoo, you're free; go explore, but come back by five."

I wander down the beach among Americans in the sand, reading, sleeping, and eating lunch in the shade. At first they don't seem too different from Cubans in the sand. But then I notice that there is no music playing and no one is dancing. This beach is quieter. Even on the beach every-thing looks very organized. Each family has their blankets, chairs, and coolers just the right distance from their neigh-bor. It looks to me like they went to a lot of trouble to relax. I wonder if I'm the only person that notices these things. Even the way the kids are playing looks different to me.

Up ahead, at the edge of the waves, a little boy and a girl are frantically shoveling, trying to save the castle that they built too close to the waves. I walk up and smile at them as I pick up an extra bucket. I fill it with sand, turn it over, and stack the sand to cover a hole in the castle walls. They do the same, and soon the wall is high enough to keep back the rippling waves. They're chattering away really fast in English. I can't understand everything they are saying but it doesn't matter because we're building a castle in the sand together.

We have just started raising the towers at each corner, when the mother sweeps down and pulls her children out of the castle. I look up at her. The sun is blazing a halo around her head, but still, I can tell she's scowling at me. As they walk away she's wagging her finger at her kids. I can't hear what she's saying, either, but I recognize the don't-play-with-strangers wag; it's the same in every language. I don't blame her; my mother would do the same thing.

I take my wrinkled shirt off and try to lie down inside the castle, but I'm too big, so I poke my legs through the walls. This is the first time I've ever felt too big to do anything. It's usually the other way around. I guess now, without my brothers trying so hard to make me feel small, I get to be as big as I want. Sometimes I miss them, but at the same time I think I like being with Angelita and Tomás better. They let me do older things, things that my brothers would say I was too young to do.

The waves are washing the castle away and my skin is starting to turn red so I run into the ocean and let the tide carry me out to the edge of the deep water. My mother or my brothers would never let me go out this far, where you can't see the bottom.

Deep down in the blue water a long shadow glides by below me just above the point where the slender shafts of light fade into blue. My brain starts scrolling through every shark story I've ever heard. At first I swim slowly so I won't splash too much, but by the time I get close to the beach, I'm sprinting.

I stumble out of the water and then throw myself down on the sand where the waves can still reach me. I make believe I'm the lone survivor of a shipwreck. After I catch my breath, I get up to explore my deserted island.

There is a strange being walking down the beach toward me. I think it's a girl but she seems to have something growing—no balanced—on top of her head. When she reaches up and adjusts the stack of palm frond hats balanced on her head, I jump up and run behind her.

"*¿Hola, tu eres Cubana?*" I say, but she doesn't stop or respond. "I see first American shark today!" I say to her in English. But she just keeps walking.

"I make hats, too—you Cuban?" I say. She stops and looks at me with a tired expression on her face. "What makes you think I'm Cuban?" she answers in Spanish.

"The hats," I say and point at the leaning tower of hats on her head.

"What about the hats?" she says and starts walking away.

I follow her to the shade of a palm where she sits down on a low wall and starts weaving four palm fronds together.

"At the camp, some of the kids made hats all day long," I say as I pick out three of the long palm fronds from her pile. "I bet that's where you learned how to make them," I say, as I weave the green spears together.

"So what?" I can tell she's not impressed. She's probably sixteen.

"We must have gone to the same camp!"

"You're nosy!" she answers as she weaves the hat into shape.

"Do you sell these? Is that how you make your living?" I ask.

"It's one of the ways."

I stick my hand out. "My name is Julian."

Her hands are surprisingly dirty. I'm not used to seeing girls with such dirty hands. Her chipped, peeling red fingernails have been chewed painfully short. "Lucia," she says, without interrupting the rhythm of her busy fingers.

"Did your parents come and get you out of the camp?"

"No, they didn't. Are you always so nosy?"

"Where do you live?"

She sweeps her stringy hair back behind her ear. "I live at a foster home on Tenth Street. They take kids in from the camps."

"I bet it's nice," I say. "At the camp if you get sent to a foster home, it usually means living with a real family in a real house. It's a lot better than getting sent to an orphanage."

She gives me a flat look. "It's not nice," she says and then grabs the weaving out of my hands. "They do it for the money." She unravels everything I did. "If you don't start it the right way, it won't end up right. Who's going to want a lopsided hat?" Her practiced fingers fold, tuck, and pull the hat into shape and then she hands it back to me.

"What do you mean they do it for the money?" I ask.

"It's like a business, they get money for every kid they take in."

"What do you mean?" I ask again.

"What I mean is that the less they spend on each kid, the more they keep for themselves. All they feed us is this weird stuff called grits, and look at the clothes they give us." She pulls at the frayed bottom of the man's plaid shirt hanging over cutoff shorts. "They buy these used at the Goodwill store, by the pound!"

"That's not fair," I say, and she shakes her head at me.

"You're telling me. One of the girls I came with was taken in by a nice rich family. She's got her own room, nice clothes, they even send her to a private school. She invited me to swim in her pool but I don't have a bathing suit, and I can't show up dressed like this!"

"Can't you tell somebody about what they're doing?"

"Look, I'm not going to sell any hats with you sitting there asking me dumb questions."

I'm trying to ignore her not-so-subtle hints. "What else do you do for money?"

"*Muy bien*, I see you are the persistent type. *Bueno*, I'll answer that question if you promise to leave me alone. Deal?"

"OK. I guess."

"Later on in the afternoon I draw pictures on the sidewalk over there." She tips her head past the big hotel behind us. "I put a cup out and the tourists throw their green dollars into it."

"They give you money for drawing? That sounds easier than carrying heavy umbrellas around."

"It's not as easy as you think. You've got to keep an eye out for Ramirez."

"Who's Ramirez?"

"He's a cop. He and his partner ride around in their big black sedan looking for runaway kids. He knows I've got a place to live, but if he's bored he'll make me stop drawing, take me back to the house, and then I can't make any money!"

"What do you do with the money?"

"One question, remember?"

"This is the last question, please?" I know when I'm being a pest. I know I'm clinging on to her but she feels, and talks, like home. She's familiar and I have no one else to talk to!

"I send it to my mother in Cuba," she says and then takes a short shallow breath like she's about to cry.

"I'm sorry," I say and put my hand on the sleeve of her shirt.

"Sorry for what? I'm all right." She moves her arm away. "My mother is buying an airplane ticket with the money to come here. Are you satisfied now?"

Now I feel ashamed of myself for bothering her.

"You have to go. Here come some customers."

"Will I see you tomorrow maybe?" I say hopefully as a couple leans in to check out the hats.

"Not if I see you first," she says.

The sun is just above the horizon by the time I finish dragging and then stacking the umbrellas next to Armando's tent. He's inside repeating the word *Connect-y-cut* over and over. When he sees me come in, he stops. "What a strange language this English." Then he pokes his head outside and checks on the umbrellas.

"*Muy bien,*" he says as he takes a handful of bills out of his pocket and puts two tens into an envelope. "Here, give this to Tomás for me. Dollars for freedom, *para la Libertad.*"

"*¿Para Libertad?*" I ask, as he hands me the envelope.

"And tell him that I talked to my brother. He and his *novia* will be ready on the twelfth."

"What are they doing on the twelfth?"

Armando looks at me and then shakes his head. "He didn't tell you?"

"Tell me what?"

"Nothing, nothing, never mind," he says and then digs deeper into his pocket.

"Here, put your hands out." Armando pours the change into my hands, and then throws in three one-dollar bills. "There, not bad for a day at the beach. See you tomorrow afternoon. Just tell Tomás I'll have the rest of his money— the money I owe him—next week."

I fold the envelope into my pocket and start walking to the bus stop. What's the money for? What are Armando's brother and his girlfriend ready for on the twelfth? I've got a funny feeling that the eleventh, circled in red on Tomás's calendar is part of the answer.

The coins in my pocket are jingling as I climb into the bus and then walk to an empty seat. We're driving down a boulevard lined with palm trees and hotels when I spot a crowd of tourists standing in a circle looking down at someone drawing on the sidewalk. When we get closer I see that it's Lucia. Tourists are dropping money into her little cardboard box. I want to get off to see what she's drawing, but I know she wouldn't be happy to see me— she's got customers.

THE PLAN

This morning the sound of an electric saw ripping into the hull wakes me up. I climb out of the cabin, look over the railing, and find Tomás fitting one of the salvaged planks into the hull of the boat. When he sees me, he waves for me to climb down and hands me one end of a plank. "Hold it in place there. Good, now push it in." He picks some rusty nails out of the bucket and starts hammering away. "I'm glad you're here." He smiles at me with four nails sticking out of his mouth.

We spend the morning replacing all of the split or rotten planks. Then while I sand the planks down to the bare wood, Tomás disappears under the tarp.

Working with Tomás is just like working with Bebo.

They never ask if I can do the job, they just show me what to do and then leave me alone. They don't doubt that I can do it and I don't, either. I like that.

Tomás comes back with three dented paint cans. "Here, I found these in the garbage." He hands me a stiff paint-brush. "Maestro, it would be an honor," he says and then points at the bare wood.

I paint the bare planks and then without asking I paint a big eye with black paint on the bow of the boat. When Tomás comes down to inspect my work, he laughs, "*El Ojo!* The Eye. It's perfect—how did you know?"

"I saw a picture of an Arawak canoe in a book once. It had an eye carved in front. The book said that the eye could see things that the people couldn't."

"You see that brass compass up there by the wheel? That's *my* eye. I paid a lot of money for it. It's the most important thing on this boat. But I guess you can never have too many eyes when you're in the middle of the ocean!" Tomás says.

We finish working late in the afternoon, and I'm hot and hungry.

"Let's go get some shrimp for dinner!" Tomás says as he puts two nets into the back of a small skiff. "Climb in." He pushes off with the oar and then starts rowing against the tide. "They're down by the last bridge," he says as he pulls on the oars.

"The shrimp swim in with the tide."

The traffic and the city are buzzing above us, but it's

peaceful down here in the green jungle water. We glide under an overhanging tree and Tomás nods at the lemons above us. "See those two babies right behind me?" he says without turning around. "Grab them. We'll make Tomás-ade tomorrow."

By the time we get to the bridge the tide has turned and is now flowing into the river. Tomás ties the boat to a piling, its bow pointing into the stream, and hands me a net. "Here, you take that side." He dips and gently swirls his net into the dark water. "The shrimp are just under the surface," he says as he lifts his net and shakes a handful of shrimp into the bucket. I try the same motion, but my net comes up empty.

By the time I figure out how to spot the ghostly shrimp and then scoop them out Tomás has already filled the bucket three-quarters full. On my last try my net comes up full.

"Now you got the hang of it." Tomás puts his net down and rows to the bank.

"We'll eat the ones you just caught," he says and picks up the bucket. "These we'll sell to the guys up on the bridge." Then he swats a mosquito off his neck. "We better hurry!"

I hold the boat as he talks to the fishermen on the bank. By the time he comes back a cloud of mosquitoes is gathering under the bridge.

"Let's get out of here!" Tomás yells as he climbs aboard.

"We've got the tide now; row us out to the middle of the channel. There's a breeze there that'll blow these little vampires away!"

Tomás taught me how to cook shrimp with rice. It tasted better than Bebo's, but I would never tell Bebo that.

Every night after dinner Tomás crosses out that day in the calendar, then he studies the tide charts and weather maps. The line of X's is getting closer to the red circle around the eleventh. Tonight he draws a blue circle that looks like the moon over the ninth of the month.

"What's that for?" I ask.

"The highest tide of the year, it's going to be a monster tide. Then the rain should start here." He draws angled blue lines from the seventh to the twelfth. "Rain, heavy rain," he says and points at a map of the tip of Florida. "This is our little river wiggling out of the Everglades. Between the rainwater draining out of the swamps and the high tide, this river is going to rise high enough to set the boat free! Just in time."

Now the numbers and circles, Armando's money, and the calendar are all starting to make sense. I bet Tomás is going back to Cuba to pick up his parents. That's his part of the deal with his father. That's why he's in such a hurry to finish his boat.

"Would that be just in time for your trip to Cuba?" I ask.

Tomás whips around. "What did that windbag Armando tell you?"

"He didn't tell me anything. He just said something about dollars for freedom. I figured out the rest by myself," I say, but he's not impressed.

Tomás paces around the cabin shaking his head. "I knew I couldn't trust him, if I didn't need his share to buy the gas, I wouldn't have let him in but I have fourteen people waiting for me."

"Are they all your family?" I ask.

"No, it's just my mother and my father. The others are people that can't get out of the country any other way. Their families have given me money to help with the boat so that I can go get them."

"How much do they have to give you?" I ask.

"They give me what they can. I would do it for nothing, but it would take much longer to make the money to fix the boat and then buy gas for the trip."

I reach deep into my pocket and pull out the ten-dollar bill the man gave me for the box of cigars, the three singles, and a handful of change from the umbrellas. "This is all the money I have. Would you bring *my* parents, too?" I ask.

Tomás stops pacing and smiles at me. "Julian, it's not that simple."

"I'll work really hard, save my money, and I can help

with the boat! You said yourself that I'm pretty good with engines! "

"Julian, this is not like going fishing. It's very dangerous. If any one of those fourteen people tells the wrong person, or if we get caught, we could all end up in jail."

"Please, Tomás, I miss my parents and they're not going to let them out—I know it."

Tomás looks away. "Julian this is a big decision for you to make for them, and us. If I let you in, I have to trust that you won't make a mistake and give it all away."

"I can keep a secret."

"You don't even know the plan." Tomás throws his pencil down on top of the charts. "It's stuffy in here and I can't think. Let's go down to the river."

There's a full, silvery moon glowing behind us in a cloudless sky. At the river's edge Tomás bends over to inspect a piece of rope sticking out of the mud. "It's all in the timing," he says as he pulls on the muddy rope. "We get to Havana as the sun is setting, when their fishing boats are returning, sneak into the harbor with them, and then tie up on the *Reglas* side. Then at sunrise we follow the first ferry across to the Havana dock."

"I know that ferry!" I say as if he had just mentioned the name of a friend. "My father keeps his fishing boat just on the other side of that dock!"

Tomás nods and continues. "He picks up his people, and then I pick up my people—the fourteen that just happen to

miss the first ferry. If they ask them why they're not taking that ferry they'll say that they're waiting for someone
and that they'll take the next one. Then we sneak out with
the other fishing boats and make a run for it!"

"That's a pretty good plan!" I say.

"That's the only way I could think of to get all those
people together with their bags and things on a dock
without the police getting suspicious."

"It sounds perfect to me."

"Every plan sounds foolproof, Julian, until you start.
Then the thousand and one things you didn't think about
go wrong—all at the same time."

"What do you do then?" I ask.

"Well then you have to improvise—invent."

"What if the floodwaters don't lift the boat?" I ask
Tomás, as he cleans his knife in the water.

"I have fourteen people counting on me. If I have to, I'll
lift the boat myself." He cuts the rope. "So do you think
your parents would do it? Are they up for an adventure?"

I look back across the gray muck at the peeling wooden
hull of the boat. Now the boat doesn't look as big or as sea-
worthy as it did before. "I think so," I say, trying to sound
more confident than I am. "My brother Alquilino said if my
mother really knew what was happening to us here, she
would swim here if she had to."

When Tomás finishes coiling up the rope he seems to
have made up his mind. "OK, they can come, but you have
to listen closely to my instructions. First you have to be

very careful about what you say when you call them because the government listens in on calls from the United States."

Tomás explains in great detail where they have to go and when they have to be there, and the password they have to use. This is a lot more complicated than I thought, but I just nod and try not to look too worried. It was so much easier when my brothers made all the decisions and I just followed them around. Now I start wondering if I'm doing the right thing for my parents. What if they get caught or the boat sinks? Am I doing this because I miss them, or do I just want to be the hero, the one who helped them to escape?

Tomás wouldn't do it to be a hero. He's doing it to keep his word—to do the right thing.

I bend over next to Tomás, cup my hands, and scoop up the water just like he does. A glowing reflection of the moon, the size of a Ping-Pong ball, floats in the palm of each hand. I lay the little moons back into the water, watching as they swim toward each other, in a hurry to be together again. I want my family to be together again. That's the only thing that I'm sure of.

MAKING TOMÁS-ADE

Tomás is still thumping around the cabin when I wake up the next morning. I watch him stack his charts and clear the counters. He's organizing, thinking. "*Buenos días*, Tomás."

"*Hola*, Julian." He takes out a beautiful brass compass from the cabinet, and gently places it on the counter. "Isn't this a beauty?" he says proudly and then wipes the domed top with his sleeve. "This is the only new piece of equipment I've bought for this boat. My father always said that you should never scrimp on the compass."

I get up to take a closer look. "Where did you get it?" I ask.

"Pops, the guy at the pumps, gave me a good deal on it.

He has a marine goods store right on the dock; someone ordered it and never picked it up," he says, then picks up four brass nuts and a shiny metal wrench from a bowl and starts up the stairs. "Come up with me. I'm going to put it in today."

Tomás clears off a place behind the wheel, then carefully lines up the four holes on the bottom of the compass with the bolts sticking out of the dash.

"Are you going to help Armando with the umbrellas today?" he asks as he slides a washer onto the bolt and then threads a nut.

"Armando doesn't need me in the morning; he just wants me to take them down in the afternoon."

"You have the morning free then?"

"Yeah, I can go with you to the tomato fields and help with the Toma-Tron. I can tune it up for you again."

"You could come with me but I've got something better for you to do!" He puts down his silver wrench and then walks down into the cabin and comes back out with two large beach bags. "If you go get the oranges, we can make Tomás-ade tonight. Then tomorrow morning you can go sell it on the street. You'll make more money there in one morning than a whole day of picking tomatoes. If it's ok with you, that money can be your contribution to the trip. Whatever you earn will go to help get your parents out."

"Of course it's OK," I answer.

"Good, this won't take long. After you finish you can

help Armando in the afternoon. I'll show you where to go to get the oranges." He sketches out the directions on a piece of a brown paper bag.

After Tomás leaves, I follow his penciled arrows, matching the names on the street signs to the ones he wrote on the paper in his clear engineer's hand. When I get to the red *X* I'm standing at the entrance ramp of a highway. There's no *X* and not one orange tree in sight but I know this has to be it. Tomás drew the map.

At the traffic light cars are jostling for position like it's the beginning of a race. An eighteen-wheeler jumps for the green light and then hurtles toward me, twin plumes of black smoke rising from the exhaust stacks. The driver pulls on his air horn, the truck tips slightly as it turns into the ramp and bushels of fresh plump oranges hiccup out of the open top. The oranges bounce on the pavement and then roll into the gutter. The driver gives me another blast from the horn and speeds up the ramp. I can see his red face in the rearview mirror. He's smiling as I run over and begin filling my bag.

One more truck goes by and my two bags are brimming with oranges.

After I drop off the oranges at the boat, I hurry back up the hill to catch the bus to the beach. On the way into the city I try to figure out how I'm going to break the news to my parents. How am I going to tell them where and when to go without giving the plan away? There might be someone listening in on the call.

By the time I've collected and stacked all the umbrellas, I think I know what to say to get them to the dock.

I'm still rehearsing my code words as I run into the tent to get my money. I'm jumpy, in a hurry to make my first phone call, but Armando wants me to listen to him read out loud in English. I try to pay attention, but after thirty seconds of his heavy accent and the mangled words, I have no idea what he's reading about.

When he finishes he asks me what I thought of his reading.

I shrug. "I don't..." but Armando is not really interested in what I think. It would make no difference to him if he were reading to a chair.

"Maybe could be better, but I think it was very good," he says with his heavy accent. He finally reaches for the money can, pours out the change into my hand and then adds two bills.

"*Gracias*, Armando," I say and then disappear through the flap.

The monkey man is talking to one of the maids over by the front desk as I sneak into the lobby. I scoot from column to column until I get to the phone booths. Making sure not to close the door so the light stays off, I sit down and then dial the number for the international operator. When she comes on I pump my quarters into the slot, and then wait in the dark. Finally the operator announces that she's made the connection and I hear the faint but familiar ringing tones. One, Two, Three, then...

"*¡Hola!*" The woman's voice sounds like it's nine hundred miles away from my ear, not the ninety miles that separates me from my house.

"This is Julian. I want to talk to my mother or my father." I feel a knot starting to form in my throat. This is the first time I have spoken those words in a long time.

"Julian. I don't know any Julian. You must have the wrong number," the woman says.

"No, no! Don't hang up please. I'm calling from the United States. I don't have any more money and I have to talk to my parents."

"Your parents? Oh! You mean the *gusanos* that used to live here?"

"*Gusanos*?" Now I recognize the voice at the other end.

It seems like a hundred years ago but I can picture her face, remember her pointing the pork chop at us like it was yesterday.

"What did you do with my parents?" I yell into the receiver.

"*Mira, niño,* I don't know what those Yankees are stuffing into your head. We have not done anything to your parents. This house is too big for just two people. They don't live here anymore." Then she barks, "*Stupido,* I told you, dig to the left!"

"Do you know where they are? Did they leave a telephone number?"

"No! *Sí*! Right there by the kitchen door."

I can barely make out what she's saying because someone is hammering away in the background.

"Do you have their number?" I yell into the receiver. I don't think she can hear me. "What's that noise? It sounds like you're digging up our floor!"

"We're digging . . ." The woman stops, but the hammering continues.

"*Caramba*, why didn't I think of it before?" she yells. "You lived in this castle! You can tell me where they buried the money, their jewels—you know—the things they should have handed over to the government when they left."

I'm almost sure they didn't bury anything. I would have known about it if they did, but maybe if I play along she'll help me find my parents.

"The money?" I ask.

"Si, *querido*. I'll tell you where your parents are, if you tell me where the money is." Even over the pounding noise, her fake sweet voice is making me sick.

I swallow hard. "OK, but you go first."

"Look my little *gusano*, this house is going to look like a piece of Swiss cheese when I get through with it, but I'll find their loot eventually whether you tell me or not. On the other hand you might never see your parents again, and that would be so sad!"

"It's under the . . ."

"Where?"

"Under the kitchen sink," I blurt out. "They lifted up a tile, and then dug a really deep hole."

"How deep?" she asks but then I hear her yell, "*En la cocina*. Dig under the sink."

"Can you tell me where my parents are now, please?"

"I'm so sorry, *gusanito*, but I have no idea where they are. They could be living out on the street just like we did before the revolution." Then she yells, "*En la cocina!*" There's a loud *click*, then a hum, and I'm left sitting in the dark, listening to the dial tone, wondering where my parents could be.

I walk out of the cool lobby and sit down in the blazing sun. I hug my knees and stare out at the sea. This sea is much darker and wilder than my sea. This sun is different, too. It stings my skin, and its light is too sharp and clear for daydreamers. But I guess that's good because it helps me see things clearly.

I take out my little notebook and look through the list of relatives and friends that my mother made for me. I'll call every number until I find them. It's not going to be easy but just like Tomás, I won't give up—no matter what!

That night after dinner, we cut and squeeze the oranges, lemons, and limes for the Tomás-ade.

Tomás puts the squeezed-out skins into a shopping bag.

"Thanks, Tomás," I say and then grab the bag. "Here, I'll get rid of these." I am afraid he will ask me if I got through to my parents so I run out of the cabin as fast as I can. I don't want to tell him yet that they aren't living at home anymore. What if he gives their place in the boat to someone else?

SELLING TOMÁS-ADE

In my dream my brothers let me go with them to the beach. We sit in the warm sand as the big land crabs crawl out of their holes to dance in the moonlight. A man and a woman are walking at the water's edge toward us. They look familiar but it isn't until they are right in front of us that I recognize them.

"Mami! Papi!" I shout as Tomás shakes me awake.

"*Buenos dias, amigo.*"

"I was dreaming about my parents," I say and look away.

"You were calling them in your sleep," Tomás says.

"I guess they snuck up on me when I was asleep."

"It's not fair that you can't control your dreams," he says, and winks at me.

"When I'm awake I can concentrate real hard on what I'm doing, then I don't think about them," I say.

Tomás rubs his chin. "I know what you mean; that's why I try to stay busy all the time."

After breakfast we tie a small folding table and a cooler to a set of wheels that once belonged on a folding shopping cart. He uses the extra rope to make a handle on one of the sides of the table. "Now you got something to hang on to."

"They'll let me take this on the bus, right?" I ask.

"No problem. I've gotten even bigger things past the bus driver. Just smile as you go by," Tomás says as we pull it up the hill and then walk to the gas station to buy ice.

"By the time you get there, the Tomás-ade will be nice and cold," Tomás says as he carefully packs the ice around the jugs in the cooler. Then he shakes my hand and wishes me luck. I wobble down the road, each wheel insisting on going in its own direction.

The bus stop is just a few steps away when a dark sedan drives by really slow. Inside the car, two men in black are scanning the empty lots in between buildings on either side of the road. I can feel their eyes behind the dark sunglasses raking over me. I wonder if that's Ramirez, the cop who drives around picking up runaway kids.

I jerk my cart into the high grass on the side of the road, lay it down and then crawl under it. My junky old table should blend in with the trash in the empty lot, but I'm thinking that they're going to hear my heart, beating as loud as the squawking of a police radio. When they stop by the bridge, one of the men gets out and looks downstream in the direction of the boat. Finally he gets back into the car and they drive off. I wait under the table until I'm sure they're not coming back. I dust myself off, then bump my table and cooler back on the sidewalk. As I walk toward the bus stop, I'm wondering why the man looked down the river. Was he looking for Tomás's boat? Angelita is the only one at the camp that knows I'm here.

By the time I reach the bus stop I'm sure that Caballo somehow made Angelita confess and now Ramirez is looking for me.

When the bus door wheezes open I lift my table up the steps, climb in, and then drop two dimes into the clinking counting machine. Sliding past the driver as smooth as I can, I walk to the back of the bus, my eyes glued to the ground so that nobody can identify me.

At my stop I walk to the back door of the bus and check one more time for the black sedan. The coast is clear so I drop my cart onto the sidewalk.

Angelita and I walked down this street on the day that I ran away from the camp. That was a week ago and already the street looks very different. In place of the building they were tearing down there is a Tinkertoy steel frame rising for a new one. The one they were working on at the other end of the street is finished, and now draped with banners and signs announcing its grand opening. The mannequins are still in the store window but now they're wearing clothes. If it weren't for the bikes and the new paint smell I wouldn't be so sure that I was on the right street.

I set up my table behind the bicycles, far enough from the street to be hidden, and still keep an eye out for Ramirez's car.

The businessmen scurrying by on the sidewalk are too busy to stop. The tourists squint at my crooked hand-writing and then walk by. I'm wondering what I'm going to do with my warm, watery Tomás-ade when a woman wearing a feathered hat stops in front of my table. Her white poodle sniffs at my knee as she opens her purse. I pick up a cup to pour out my first drink but she shakes her head.

"You poor thing," she says and then drops a dollar bill into my cup.

"Poor thing?" Before I can ask her what she means, she yanks on her poodle and then walks away.

"I think poor means *pobre,*" I say out loud to the stream of people flowing around me in their hats and flowered shirts. Across the street in a store window, the boy in the dirty T-shirt and crumpled shorts just stands there holding his cup. I wave at the reflection, and it waves back.

"Hey kid, you selling drinks or posing for pictures?" A construction worker asks as three of his buddies grab cups from my stack. "Is this self-serve, or you pour?"

"I no poor!" I say indignantly.

"OK, kid, you're not poor. Don't get huffy, we've all been there!" The man laughs. A group of guys in dusty yellow hard hats crowd in and start pouring themselves glass after glass of Tomás-ade. I don't even have to ask for money; they keep dropping dimes and quarters into my cup, as they stand around my table telling jokes and looking at the pretty office girls walking by.

When their coffee break is over, both of my jugs are empty, and my cup is full. They pat me on the back as they head back to work and make me promise to come back tomorrow.

I pack up the cooler and the table as quick as I can, check for Ramirez, and then roll across the street to cool off in the big department store.

I pull my squeaking cart down an aisle crowded with car parts, lawn furniture, and clothes—mostly things that I've never seen before. I can't even read the labels so I just let my eyes swim across the shelves, but when I spot the big colored chalks, I stop. They look like the ones that my mother gave me in Cuba. There are twelve colors inside. I turn the box over and over thinking that one dollar and thirty-nine cents is a lot of money, but then I remember Lucia and the tourists throwing money into her cup. I'm sure I can get them to throw just as many coins in my cup.

As I walk to the beach I'm thinking about what I'm going to draw: palm trees, boats, blue skies, and clouds or maybe El Morro, the fort at the entrance of Havana Harbor.

I cross the boulevard and find a shady spot where there are plenty of people walking by and the sidewalk is not too rough. I open up my box of chalks, tip my head, and then pace around the square of sidewalk.

A vague and familiar shape is rising out of the gum spots and soda stains on the cement. Kneeling down, I draw my first line. It curves into a circle, and there is the nostril of a horse. I flesh out his muzzle, then flash along the arc of his neck all the way to the flying tail. I make my way back along the belly, up and down the legs. Now the horse is running. I erase the bumps and shapes that don't look right and then fill in the muscles that I do know. I put the bit in the horse's mouth and follow the reins to the boy's hand, to the arm, chest, and then the neck and the head. As I color in the patch of blue sky and puffy clouds behind the rider, coins start raining down around me.

When I finish I scramble around the sandy feet in flip-flops collecting quarters and dimes, smiling up at the *turistas* at the same time. I'm reaching for a dollar bill when the tip of a black shoe pins it to the sidewalk. I tug hard, but the shoe won't let go.

"*¡Mi peso!*" My dollar, I yell at the man on the other end of the shoe. I wonder why someone would be wearing a black suit at the beach? How could I be so careless? I glance up and see the badge and a name tag pinned to his lapel. It says, Officer Ramirez. I'm in trouble.

"*¿Como te llamas?*" Ramirez asks and takes out a little notebook.

"Uh—uh, Jorge?" I mutter.

"Jorge?" he asks and then lifts his foot.

I fold the bill into my pocket. "*Sí*, Jorge."

"And where do you live, Jorge?"

I hesitate for a moment "The foster home on Tenth Street," I say, hoping I got it right.

"I know that place. I'll bet you came with Pedro Pan, right?"

"*Sí, sí*, that's what it said on the name tag."

"What's your last name Jorge?" he asks.

But I can't think of a name. He taps on his notebook with his pencil.

"Last name?" he says patiently.

"Ra-Ramirez. I mean Gonzales," I mumble, I can feel myself turning red.

The other man in the dark sedan parked at an odd angle to the curb calls out, "Hey, Ramirez, I'm hungry!"

Ramirez snaps his notebook shut, and then waves it at me. "*Muy bien*, Jorge Ramirez-Gonzales. I'll check this out." Ramirez is halfway back to the car when he turns around and lifts up his sunglasses so I can see his eyes. "*Cuidate, Cubanito.*"

Ramirez-Gonzales? He caught me by surprise. I should have had it all worked out. But I guess it doesn't really matter what name I give him. When he checks at the foster home he'll know, and then he'll come looking for me.

As I pull my cart down the road I tell myself that next time I'll be ready. I'll see Ramirez before he sees me and then dump the cart and run. He'll never catch me. But it's a shame that I won't be able to come back here. Just one picture and I have enough money to make two phone calls, with some left over for Tomás. The only place that I can think of where it'll be safe to draw is the hotel. Maybe if I talk to the monkey man he'll let me draw by the pool.

As I walk to the bus I duck into the first phone booth I pass and try my father's office number. The man who answers the phone recognizes my father's name but then he announces that the only reason he knows the name is because it's printed in gold on the door.

"Do you know where he could be?"

"How could I know where he is? I never met the man!" he says and hangs up.

The next number on the list has been disconnected. I've made three calls and nothing. This is a lot harder than I thought it would be.

MONSTER ENGINE

I climb up the ladder and find the deck littered with wires and greasy engine parts.

"We'll turn her over as soon as I get this nice and tight," Dog yells from inside the engine compartment. He's tightening the four bolts at the bottom of the carburetor. Tomás is standing by the wheel. "*Hola*, Julian," he says.

Dog looks up with a lopsided smile creeping across his face and I notice that his canines are very pointy. They're too long for a human, or even a dog, but not for a wolf.

"What are you looking at?" he grunts at me.

"Oh, nothing." I must have been staring.

"Pass me that wrench by your foot," he says.

"What are you doing?" I ask as I kick it over.

"I got Tomás some new parts for his engine," Dog says.

"Dog, you know as well as I do those parts are used," Tomás yells back.

"Almost new," Dog barks.

Tomás turns toward me. "He thinks just because he puts them in boxes he found in back of a garage, I'll pay him for new parts." He laughs. "I wasn't born yester-day, Dog."

"Now that we're on the subject," Dog says as he climbs out of the engine compartment, "I got to get out of the river before the tide changes. If you've got my money . . ."

"Sure, I'll go get it," Tomás says, then steps into the cabin.

I watch Dog walk to the wheel. There's something about him that I don't like, something that I don't trust. He's checking out Tomás's compass, I hear him say under his breath, "This is a mighty tight piece of equipment." Then he leans in to study the bolts holding it in place.

He must have sensed that I was watching him because he whips around and locks me in his yellow wolf eyes. "Why you looking at me like that?" He growls low so that Tomás can't hear him. "If I were you, I wouldn't go around sticking my nose where it don't belong."

Just then Tomás comes out with the money can and starts counting out a handful of bills.

"Now, this compass was bought new. Right?" Dog says changing his tone.

Tomás hands him the money. "That's my pride and joy."

"Must a cost a pretty penny, too!" Dog comments as he

slowly inspects it from its shiny dome down to the four bolts securing it behind the wheel.

"I can still count on you for the trip? We leave on the eleventh."

"Sure, Tomás, as long as you can pay me, you can count on me."

I wait for Dog to start up the outboard motor on his skiff to ask Tomás, "Why do you trust Dog?"

"Why not?"

"I wouldn't trust that guy. I don't like him."

"I don't have to trust him, Julian. You heard him; I just have to make sure I can pay him."

"I saw him checking out your compass—what if he steals it?"

"Julian, I've been around boats all my life and I've met a lot of guys like Dog. I know he's not my friend, but he's not a crook." Tomás sounds angry.

"Sorry, Tomás, but I have this feeling."

"You can't go around calling people crooks, just because you have a feeling."

"There's just something about him. I would never trust a guy like that; he looks like a wolf to me."

"Oh, I see, now. It's because of the way he looks." Tomás is laughing at me. "Just pass me that wrench please."

We stayed up late trying to put in the new-used parts. When I finally tumbled into bed, I was so tired that I didn't even bother to wash up. Why wash up if you're just going to get dirty again? As I drift off I can hear Tomás still tinkering with the carburetor up on deck. He's determined to get the engine started tomorrow.

∧∧

I wake up to the roar of the engine; the ribs and bones of the boat are shaking; the bunk is vibrating.

"All hands on deck!" Tomás yells.

When I stumble out there's a cloud of exhaust hanging over the deck, but the engine is quiet.

"You see the red wires by the wheel? When I give you the signal, connect them. Red to red," he says.

I stub my toe on the bucket of nails, and then limp to the bundle of red and white wires slithering out from behind the peeling dashboard. Tomás makes his final adjustments, then calls out, "Fire her up!"

A yellow and blue spark flies across the gap between the red wires as Tomás scrambles over the groaning engine, feeding it gas, adjusting screws.

"Try it again!" he says.

The engine spews blue smoke again, and then dies. I watch Tomás trying to adjust the carburetor. "That carburetor looks older than the one that we had on our boat, and Bebo said that it was ready for the trash heap." Tomás doesn't look up. I can't figure out why Tomás can't see the wolf in Dog's face. He might be smart about inventing machines that bounce tomatoes around and fixing up boats, but he sure isn't too smart about people.

"Get back to the wires. We're almost ready," Tomás says.

I grab the bundle of wires and he yells, "Go ahead!"

When I connect the red wires the engine roars to life. It's running rough, like it's about to shake itself into a thousand pieces.

"She's going to blow! Shut her off!" Tomás yells.

I pull the wires apart; the engine sputters and dies.

"Great! Did you hear that?" Tomás sings as he dances around the deck. "It won't be long now."

ARMANDO'S SURPRISE

It took a few days but I convinced monkey man to let me draw on the path to the beach; the only problem is that I have to give him half of the money I collect. It made me mad at first because I'm doing all the work and it's not even his hotel, but I have no choice. Ramirez never comes here.

Today I drew a picture of a big marlin fish jumping and a tiny fisherman, half its size, looking determined to pull the big fish into the boat. It looks just like the one painted on the plate that I broke. The tourists seemed to like it so I went to the other side of the pool and drew another one.

After I collect the two dimes and three nickels, I go find the monkey man. He insists that I empty my pockets in front of him so that he can count the money himself.

"Why, do you think I would cheat you?" I say.

"Wouldn't you?" he says.

As he counts the money I realize that I did the same thing to Dog, and that's why Tomás got mad at me. I guess I just assumed he looked like a crook. But still I think I'm right about Dog and the monkey man is wrong about me.

Monkey man counts and then divides it up. He stacks most of the coins on his side. "I need the coins to make change," he says as he gives me a few coins and two one-dollar bills.

I scoop up my half of the money, and count the change. I have enough to make one short call. When he leaves I sneak around to the phone booth and sit down inside. I look over my numbers, trying to decide which one to call. On the back cover of my notebook I find a number written in a different hand than my mother's. Now I remember that Bebo wrote that number down on the last day that I talked to him in the kitchen. It's his mother's number. He said he was going to stay with her while he was waiting for school to start.

One, two, three, four rings—I think he said that his mother lived in the country—*five, six*—and that she had a garden—*seven, eight, nine*—maybe he's ...

"*¿Hola?*"

"Bebo! I can't believe it. You're the first one, the only one. Is that really you?"

"This is really me, but the question is who are you?"

"You don't recognize my voice?" I say. "It's good to hear your voice!"

"Julian! ¿*Amigo, que dices?* I didn't recognize your voice. You sound all grown up. What are those Yankees feeding you?"

"Oh, you know, meat loaf, oatmeal—American food."

It's good to hear Bebo laugh even if he's ninety miles away.

"Bebo, have you seen my parents?"

"Chico, the last time I saw them was two weeks ago. I went to your father's office to get some things I left behind. He was moving out."

"Did he say where he was going?"

"*Sí*, he said he was going to San Miguel. They're staying in a house that we built. The guy he built it for left the country."

"Did he leave a number?" I ask.

"No, he said there's no phone there."

"No phone?" I can't believe it. "How am I going to get in touch with them?"

"I could take a bus there. What do you need to tell them?"

"You would do that for me, Bebo?"

"Of course, you're my friend, Julian. You would do the same for me."

"Tell them to go to . . ." but then I stop when I remember Tomás telling me that sometimes people listen in on calls. I've rehearsed what I was going to say but I imagined I was going to say it to my mother. What if I say something wrong and I get Bebo in trouble?

"Take your time, Julian, I understand," Bebo says calmly. I think he does understand. Bebo could always read my mind.

"Tell them Tomás's father has Mami's little bird in *Reglas* and if she wants it, she has to take the first ferry there on the twelfth," I blurt out real fast.

"That's all I need, Julian; you don't have to say anything else. I'll take care of it today. You can call me back tomorrow at the same time. So how are your brothers?" Bebo asks, changing the subject, but before I can answer I hear a click and the operator comes on to ask for more money. I know that I have no more quarters but I search my pockets anyway. Then I hear the dial tone and I know he's gone.

As I walk back to Armando's tent I don't know whether to feel happy or worried. What if Bebo doesn't find them? What if they say no? What if they say yes? What if they get caught? What if the boat sinks? My brain is stuttering on an endless list of what-ifs. I sit down in the shade of the tent. Inside I can hear Armando talking but I don't pay attention because he's always talking to himself, reciting facts or repeating words over and over like a Cuban parrot.

Then I hear Tomás's angry voice. "I need your share for the gas." I peek inside and Tomás is standing over Armando, with his fists clenched.

"Look, Tomás, I told you already, I can't do anything about it. His *novia* does not want to come, and my brother will not leave without her."

Tomás looks like he's going to hit Armando. "You promised. You gave your word!"

I close the flap. Now I'm convinced that I can't say anything about my phone call. I have to wait.

When I look inside Armando is frantically searching through his notes. "Ah jes, here it is. When a door closes, a window opens."

Tomás whirls around. "This is what I think of your window that opens!" He pulls the notes off the tent, crumples them up, and throws them out the window. "Everyone else gave me their money already." His voice is scary calm. "I let you go until the end because I trusted you, but I need every nickel that was promised. You know that I can't make the trip without it."

"Sorry, amigo, but I've already spent that money," Armando whispers as if he's letting us in on a big secret. "English lessons." Then he announces cheerfully, "They start next week!"

Tomás is rocking from side to side. It looks like he can't decide whether to rush Armando or turn around and leave. I step inside and stand in between him and Armando. "Tomás, I have some money," I say and dig my bills out of my pocket. "Here, this is for you. I have more on the boat."

Tomás puts his hands down, opens his fists, and I push the money into his hand.

Tomás looks at the folded bills. "Thank you, Julian, but I'll need a lot more than this."

I gently push him outside. "I have more on the boat. Let's go home."

When we step out onto the sand, he exhales and stares at the sea. I can feel him trying to push his anger out to the blue horizon, so it can float away with the ivory clouds. Then he inhales slowly and says, "I have to find a way."

PATCHING

We're sitting in a booth at Pirate Angel's. Tomás is working his numbers on a napkin.

"Without Armando's share, it's going to be really close," he says and then crosses out all the numbers and starts again.

Dr. De La Vega is balancing a knife on his finely tapered but pruny fingers. "Tomás, I've given you everything I have."

His boss, Mr. Papanapalulis, twists the ends of his bushy mustache and asks, "How much?"

"We need a life raft, spare spark plugs, and cables, then I have to fill both gas tanks." Tomás writes a figure on a napkin and hands it to him.

"That's a lot of money!" Mr. Papanapalulis says, and

then scratches the gray stubble on his chin. "When we come to this country from Greece many people help. That's why I hire the doctor; he's a lousy dishwasher but someday he'll be a great doctor. We all need to help sometimes so I give you twenty-five, but that's all. If my wife finds out I give you our house money"—he pulls his index finger across his throat.

Tomás shakes his hand. "Thank you, I'll pay you back as soon as I can."

The doctor puts his arm around his boss. "This is a good man! *Amigo*, when I get my doctor's license I promise to operate on any organ you want, for free!" Then he plants a loud smacking kiss on top of his shiny head. Mr. Papanapalulis quietly chews on the end of his mustache, contemplating the offer as he starts walking back to the kitchen. When he sees that the doctor is still sitting in the booth, he bangs on the counter. "Back to work!" he roars. "Remember, in Miami there are many doctors that want to wash dishes!"

As the doctor gets up he slips a ring from his finger. "My wedding ring," he says as he pushes the ring across the table toward Tomás. "You said the guy at the pumps would trade jewelry and things for gas. This will buy a few gallons."

Tomás shakes the doctor's hand. "I'll try to talk him into not selling it until I can buy it back. But I can't promise anything." Tomás gets up. "*Gracias, amigo*. Someday I will repay your kindness. "

The doctor shrugs his shoulders. "Amigo, all we can do is try," he says and then slides out of the booth.

"Good-bye, Julian."

Tomás is already heading for the door.

"Good-bye, Doctor. Good luck with your tests," I say and then hurry to catch up with Tomás.

"It's starting to rain," I yell, but Tomás doesn't answer. He must be juggling miles, dollars, and gallons of gas in his head. As I run to catch up, I see a dark sedan idling by the curb. The two men inside are looking straight at us.

"Tomás," I yell, "it's Ramirez, the guy in the car. He's a policeman. We've got to run!"

When he sees the car, Tomás snaps out of his numbers trance and pulls me into the driveway of a used car lot. "¡Caramba! That's all I need now. Don't look at them. Don't run until I tell you," he whispers, as we walk past the sales trailer. "Stay low and head for the vans. They won't see us there."

We duck down low and run in between the sedans toward the tall vans in the back of the car lot. I can see the back fence but then a large man in a black plastic raincoat jumps out from behind a van and blocks our path.

"Hey! What are you doing here?" he yells in English.

Tomás dives to the right and I run to the left. Tomás is one step ahead, so the man grabs me instead. I'm kicking and squirming as the giant lifts me up over his head and starts running back to his trailer by the road. From up here I can see over the tops of the vans and the dark sedan just turning into the lot. I look down, and Tomás is running toward us with a broom. He pokes the broom handle in between the man's legs. The man stumbles, lets go, and now I'm flying through the air. I land and then bounce back up on my feet. The man is trying to get up but his legs are tangled up in his raincoat. Tomás throws the broom at him and then I follow Tomás to the fence.

As we negotiate the sharp barbs on top of the chain-link fence, the men in the black suits are jumping over the giant.

We twist and slide our way through a tangle of thorny bushes. Ripe, red berries stain our clothes and skin, as a squawking blue jay, angry that we've disturbed its banquet, dives and pecks at our heads.

"We're on the wrong side of the river," Tomás groans.

We dive in and start swimming across. Tomás is way ahead of me when the strong current in the middle of the river grabs me. I swim as hard as I can but I still end up downstream from the boat.

Tomás is waiting for me inside the cabin when I trip down the steps and, before I can say anything, he pounds his fist on the counter. "You didn't tell me that they're looking for you, Julian."

"Why? They're not looking for you, Tomás," I say.

"Julian, if they caught us just now they would have dragged me in with you! Even if I got away they would come after me."

"Why? You didn't do anything!"

"First thing they'll ask you is where are you living?" Tomás waves his hand around the cabin. "When they come down here they'll know right away what I'm up to. If the Coast Guard takes my boat away, what do you think is going to happen to all those people waiting on the dock? I told you right from the beginning, the more people in the chain the riskier it gets. One little mistake, one weak link, and we all sink. "

I look away hoping he won't ask me about my parents. If I told him that I had to leave a message with Bebo he would see it as one more link in the chain. He wouldn't understand that Bebo is my friend. I trust him.

Tomás doesn't say more than three words to me for the rest of the afternoon. We work late into the night clearing the decks, checking off the things on his long list that have to be done before he can leave. He was still up when I went to bed.

RAIN

In the morning, I step out into the rain and watch the brown waters climbing up the bank. If it keeps raining, the boat will soon float, just as Tomás predicted.

Tomás is on the bank hauling his treasures out from under a tarp, making a pile of the things he will need up on deck: ropes, spare parts, cans, and hoses.

"Let's get out of the rain," he says, and then guides me down into the cabin.

"You haven't said anything about your parents. I guess that means that you couldn't find them."

"Well, maybe they might—"

Tomás cuts me off. "Save it. I don't have time for maybes. Julian, you should have said something a long time ago."

"I'm waiting to hear from them . . ."

"I don't have time for excuses; I've got too many other things to worry about. If your parents are at the dock on time they can come." Then Tomás takes some bills out of the money can and grabs his raincoat. "Right now I have to go buy enough gas to get the boat to the pumps and I'll use the rest to buy some spare parts and fill up the tanks. You stay here while I'm gone. I don't want you getting picked up by that Ramirez guy."

"But I have one more call to make! And even if he did pick me up, I would never tell him about the boat."

"I can't take any more chances," he says as he climbs down the ladder. "And, Julian, when this boat leaves, you have to go back to the camp."

"But Caballo . . ."

"I don't want to hear it. The camp is where you belong." Then Tomás starts up the slippery bank. Halfway up he stops and turns around. "By the way, Dog is coming later in the afternoon. If I'm not back by then tell him to wait, because we're leaving today—no matter what." I watch Tomás pull himself up the muddy bank and then disappear into the bushes that line the road.

I can't be mad at Tomás; he's got a job to do—fourteen people are depending on him. He's like Bebo; when he's in a bind, he only thinks about what's in front of him, what he has to do. He doesn't worry about the things, good or bad, that put him in that spot.

I have a job to do, too. I'll make my call and come right back. Tomás has nothing to worry about.

It's too early to make my call, so I go below, open up my suitcase, and start folding my damp clothes. When I finish packing I run my hand along the side where the golden swallow is still sleeping. Just as I close my suitcase I hear the drone of an outboard motor coming up the river.

Dog is maneuvering past the submerged dock to tie his skiff to a log on the bank. I can hear him cursing the slippery mud as he makes his way to the ladder.

As I walk out of the cabin, Dog is leaning over the compass and facing away from me.

"Hi, Dog," I say, loud enough to startle him.

Dog jumps back and turns around to glare at me. "What are you doing here?" he asks as he jams something long and metallic into his pocket.

"You're here early, aren't you?" I ask.

"I'm just helping my buddy Tomás out. You know—a thousand things to do to get ready." Dog smiles and then starts fumbling with the wires.

"Tomás wanted me to tell you that he's leaving today, no matter what. He wants you to wait for him."

"I'm all ready to go," Dog says, then grabs a roll of electrical tape. "I better get started wrapping these. We don't want them to unravel in the middle of the ocean."

Standing behind him, I watch him tape up the wires. Maybe I was wrong to assume that he's up to no good.

Maybe he is just a guy trying to earn some money to fix his boat like Tomás said.

Suddenly, Dog turns around. "Don't you have anything better to do?"

"Sorry," I say, and then pick up the broom and start sweeping the deck. After I finish the deck, I go down to the cabin to sweep and reorganize the food in the galley. When it's time to go Dog is still taping up the loose wires.

"I've got to go up and make a phone call. I'll be back soon," I say as I walk past him.

Dog looks up and smiles. "You take your time. I'll stand watch." I stop when I see his big yellow canines.

"I think I forgot something," I blurt out as I dive back into the cabin. I reach under the counter, grab the money can, take all the bills out, and jam them in my pocket. As I walk out on deck again, Dog's still smiling.

"It's the teeth," I say to myself as I climb up the hill.

BAD NEWS

The rain and the tide have raised the river to the third rung on the ladder and waist deep. I wade to shore then climb up the muddy, slippery bank to the road. Before I step across the bridge I look up and down the wet road for Ramirez. The coast is clear so I run all the way to the closest phone, right outside Pirate Angel's. I look around again one more time and then start dialing.

When a woman answers, I ask for Bebo. "He's out fixing a car," she says.

"This is Julian. Did he say when he will be back?"

"*Sí, hola,* Julian. He had an emergency repair out on the highway but he left a message for you just in case he didn't get back in time." I hear the clunk of the receiver being set down, then the shushing of her sandals on the tiles. "Here it is. He wrote it down." I can hear her mumbling, mouthing the words before she reads them. "'They were there, but now they are not.'" She reads each syllable slowly. "'Sorry, Bebo.'"

"Where is he going to check? There has to be more!" I say.

"That's all he wrote," she says.

"I have nothing left," I say and then hang up. What's the use?

The rain is coming down in sheets when I step outside. The soaking rain is pushing me down and my shirt feels like it's made out of lead. I feel like I have nothing left to push back with. I must have been crazy to believe that it would work, that someone like me could make something this big and important happen.

I'm standing ankle deep in a puddle that looks as big as a sea. The reflection of the red Pirate Angel sign is flashing in the shallow water. Even upside down the lady pirate's face reminds me of Angelita. I can almost feel her hand reaching out to me.

Suddenly the red reflection shatters into a thousand little rubies as a car skids to a stop right in front of me. A man jumps out of the dark sedan but I can't run—my legs have turned to wood. He grabs my arm and pulls me to the car but he's having a hard time folding my wooden body into the backseat.

The driver is getting annoyed. "Ramirez, do I have to do everything myself?"

"It's not my fault, boss. He won't bend!" Ramirez answers and then he says to me, "*Mira, chico*, a little cooperation—we're here to help you! The camp called us when you ran away. Your mother is here. She's worried sick about you. We're here to take you back."

"*¿Mi madre?*" He must be talking about someone else's mother. My mother disappeared. She's never at the other end of the line when I call.

"*Vamos, niño*, your mother is waiting for you," Ramirez croons as he pulls me gently into the backseat.

How do I know he's not saying that just to get me into the car? As I slide into the backseat his partner turns around. He's holding a piece of paper with what looks like my passport picture on it. "That's him all right," he says and hands the paper to Ramirez.

Ramirez glances at it and then slams the door. "Julian, we're taking you back to where you belong."

"Where I belong?" I mumble as a swirling fog creeps over me, leaving me numb and too tired to lift my arms.

Ramirez is leaning over me. "*¿Que dices?*"

When I look at him I feel like I'm seeing things through a rolled-up newspaper. Little details pop up like the black hairs bristling out of Ramirez's nose. Then I notice the little birds—I think they're swallows—flying on his red tie.

"The swallow, red rubies," I say as if I'm in a trance and Ramirez shakes his head at me.

I jerk my head back as if someone has just slapped me awake. "My suitcase!" I yell, and Ramirez jumps back.

"Suitcase?" Ramirez asks. "Tell us where it is, we'll take you there."

"Take me there?" I can't take him to the boat; he'll arrest Tomás and then fourteen people will ... and then it hits me. I have the gasoline money! All those people waiting on the dock for Tomás, my mother counting on me to protect the bird so we'll have some money to start a new life. I've let everyone down!

The seat is trying to suck me in. "I can't let everybody down!" I say out loud.

Ramirez gives me a strange look. "I think we better get him back, *pronto*," he calls out to the driver and then slams the door.

There's a man fishing off the bridge. As we drive by, he turns around. The shape of his head silhouetted against the silver clouds reminds me of Bebo. He would want me to try; he wouldn't just sit back and let things happen!

Suddenly, I feel the fog is lifting and I know exactly what I have to do.

"Stop the car!" I yell as loud as I can. "I'm going to be sick, really sick!"

Ramirez looks at me as if I'm possessed, then slides all the way to the other end of the seat. The driver looks back and then slows down. I push the door open and tumble out of the car. Ramirez is still holding on to my hand. I hit the ground running but I fall and scrape my knees. Ramirez sees that I'm getting dragged, so he lets go. Ramirez is running after me but I reach the bridge first.

Climbing up on the railing, I look out over the buzzing highway, the rooftops and then out to sea. This time I'm not going to look down. It's only ninety miles to Havana from here, but a very long drop to the muddy water below.

GRAVITY SLIPS

When I jump, Ramirez grabs my foot. *"Tu madre,"* he
yells. "She's waiting." For a second gravity slips and the
blue sky holds me. I'm floating above the river, his words
snapping all around me like little banners, then the water rushes up too soon and I smack into the river face-
first.

As I swim downstream on my back, I see Ramirez leaning over the railing waving my left shoe at me. "She's waiting!" he yells again.

If the current wasn't pulling on me so hard, I might
have turned around and swum back to the bridge and let
Ramirez take me to my mother. But I know that it's just a
mean trick that he uses to catch runaways. I can't go back

yet. Right now I have to get the gas money and my bird to Tomás and I have to do it quick. I'm sure Ramirez will be looking for me along the river, and then he'll probably find the boat.

The boat is still sitting on top of the refrigerator, but now there is a stream of fast water between the hull and the bank. As I climb up on deck I see two red gas cans that weren't there when I left.

"Tomás, come out. Hurry," I call into the cabin and then look up the bank toward the highway.

Tomás walks out of the cabin holding the empty money can. "It's over, Julian, the gas money is gone." Tomás drops the can and then sits down on the deck. "You were right; I shouldn't have trusted him. I shouldn't have trusted anyone." Then he lies down.

I dig his roll of bills out of my left pocket. "Tomás, he's not a crook; I took the money just in case," I say and then I hand it to him.

Tomás sits up and points back at the wheel. "You didn't notice."

The shiny brass compass is not behind the wheel, only the four bolts are left.

"It's gone!"

"You were right. He is a crook."

"Why did he take it? He told me he has a compass just like it."

"He probably traded it for a tank of gas," Tomás says and then lies back down. "It's all over."

"Tomás, you can't give up. We've got to get it back!"

"We'd have to buy it back, Julian, and we barely have enough money for the gas we'll need for the trip."

I'm about to sit down next to him when I feel the deck slide and then tip slightly.

"Did you feel that?" I ask.

Tomás wipes the rain out of his eyes. "Feel what?"

The deck leans and then rises like a ride at the amusement park.

"Hey, she's floating!" I yell and run to look over the side. "Tomás, the water is halfway up the hull; you were right! We've still got a chance!"

Tomás joins me at the rail. "I guess I figured one thing right, but it doesn't really matter. If it was just me, alone, I would try it, but I can't risk fourteen lives. It's my fault. My father wanted to teach me to navigate by the stars, but I thought, why do I need the stars when I've got a compass?"

"Tomás, I can't believe you're giving up!" I yell and pull on his arm. "You said that you would lift the boat up yourself if you had to!"

"It's over, Julian. Now the only thing I can do is to try to get in touch with them so they won't show up at the dock," Tomás says and then nods toward the cabin. "You better go and pick up your clothes; you left them all over the cabin. Go and pack. I'll walk you to the bus stop."

"Pick up my clothes?" I rush into the cabin. My suitcase is open, my jumbled clothes dripping over the sides. "Dog!" I hope he was just looking for the gas money. I hold my breath as my fingers run along the side of the suitcase and then slow down near the corner. There's the edge; the blue lining is not cut. The bird is safe still sleeping in its little compartment.

"What are you looking for?" Tomás asks as I check the lining again.

"My mother's golden swallow, she had it sewn in there before we left. I'm supposed to guard it until my parents get here. Didn't you tell the doctor that you could buy his ring back from the guy at the pump when you got back? You could trade the bird in for your compass. You could get more gas and all the spare parts you'll need."

"I don't know, Julian. I'm sure your parents are counting on that bird for when they get here. They'll need the money to start over."

"Tomás, just give me a knife," I say and hold out my hand.

The sharp blade slices easily through the silky material, I pull it back and there it is—a tiny door. When I pry it open the sleeping bird tumbles out.

"It's here, it's really here!" I pick up my mother's golden swallow and then press it against my cheek. I can smell her perfume, see her teardrop face floating above me, hear her voice when she asked me to guard it for the family. "I hope you understand, Mami," I say, then hand the bird over to Tomás as fast as I can.

"Are you sure you want to do this?" Tomás asks as he bounces it in his hands.

"You said yourself that those people are desperate to get out and if you don't show up they'll probably get arrested. You've got fourteen people depending on you. I think it's the right thing to do," I say, trying to sound like I'm sure. I wish my mother's face wasn't floating above me, frowning at me.

"Don't you mean sixteen? Aren't your parents coming?"

"No," I say, hoping he won't ask why. If I tell him what Ramirez said about my mother being here already, he might not let me go with him. There might be a lot of things that are gray and unclear but there is one thing I am sure of: Tomás wouldn't have hired Dog to go with him if he could make the trip alone. He needs me to go with him and I want to go.

Tomás cups the bird in his hands and looks up at the peeling paint on the beams overhead. "I admire you for wanting to help," he says. "I know how much that bird means to you and your family but I have no choice. I accept your generous offer. Julian, if there's ever anything I can do for you or your family, just ask."

I was waiting for him to say that. "Yes, you can do something for me. Let me go with you."

"Julian, I have to get past the Coast Guard, motor ninety miles in this leaky tub, then sneak into Havana Harbor. No—no way, it's just too dangerous."

"I know the harbor! That's where my father kept his fishing boat. Besides, now that Dog is out you'll need someone to help with the engine," I say. Tomás shakes his head and paces across the deck. He leans over the railing to check the swiftly rising water.

"Tomás, you don't have a choice about this either," I yell and point up at the highway. "Ramirez is up there; if we don't leave right now you might never go!" Ramirez is now climbing over the railing yelling something down at us. Tomás finally looks at me. "I guess you are in," he says as Ramirez slips and slides down the muddy bank in his nice black suit.

"Ready with the bowline!" Tomás yells and then starts up the engine.

Ramirez is skating on the mud down to the shore as I untie the line from the cleat on the bow.

"Where are you going? Didn't you hear me? Your mother is waiting for you," Ramirez shouts over the roar of the engine and then pulls a piece of paper out of his pocket. "This is her letter," he waves an airmail envelope at me. "She's at your uncle's house in Connecticut!"

Now I believe him. It's not a trick. It's really her. I measure the distance from the boat to the shore. It's far, but I'm a good swimmer.

"Come back, Julian!" Ramirez says, tugging gently on the other end of the line. "Drop the rope and jump. I'll take you to her."

If I drop the rope and jump, this sad empty feeling that's been living in my chest since I left my family will go away—I know it.

But I can't just jump and leave Tomás and those people on the dock; they need me.

"Tell my mother that I love her." Then I toss my end of the line to Ramirez.

"Let's get out of here!" Tomás yells.

The vibration from the engine is buzzing up my legs like electricity as the boat nudges out into the middle of the river. I can feel the churning current pulling on the boat. We've hooked on to something even more powerful than a big fish.

As we rush under the bridge where we caught the shrimp, Tomás nudges me. "Look who's up there!" he says and points behind us. The black sedan has just stopped on the bridge. The door opens and Ramirez gets out.

The old boat is shaking as we speed out of the narrow river and into a choppy sea. Every time we slap into a wave it creaks and complains as if it's about to fall apart.

When we finally reach the gas pumps, Tomás maneuvers the boat up to the dock and jumps down to secure the stern line. "Julian, get the bowline. I'll go talk to Pops. We've got to get in and out quick. Ramirez is bound to show up here any minute."

When I walk into the marine supply store, an old guy—Pops, I guess—is sitting behind the counter already inspecting the rubies on the wings of the golden swallow. His bushy eyebrows jump halfway up his leathery forehead as he bounces it in the palm of his hand and says, "Solid."

"It's worth much money," I say and wave my hand over the growing pile of spare parts and life preservers that Tomás is hurriedly collecting. "*Mucho mas* than this."

"You're right; this is a mighty fine piece of work. The last time I saw a piece like this was in a museum," Pops says. "Son, are you sure you want to leave this with me?"

The tone of his voice makes me think maybe it's a lot more valuable than even my mother thought it was. But I guess that doesn't matter, because we are trading it for something you can't add or subtract. How can you put a price on fourteen people waiting on a dock?

Tomás comes back with a rubber raft and a used compass cradled in his arms. "This stuff and two tanks of gas is all we need," he says. "But you have to promise to give me one month to make the money to buy it back."

"Tomás, you know me. I never promise nothing, but I always do my best." He chuckles, and then shuffles out to the pumps.

While Pops fills the gas tanks, I bolt the used compass back on behind the wheel and try to keep an eye out for Ramirez at the same time. Tomás puts away the spare parts and then disappears into the cabin.

I make sure the compass is secure and then go below. Tomás is bending over a chart pointing at the end of a familiar chain of islands hooking south from the tip of Florida. "This is where we'll wait," he says.

"That's Key West. It's ninety miles to Havana from there," I say, and Tomás looks up, surprised. "We had a chart just like this one on our boat," I explain. "Bebo was teaching me how to read it before we left. Why do we have to wait?"

"We can't wait here. Ramirez might just show up any

minute but if we leave now, we'll get to Havana too early. We'll motor south, keeping the Keys close to the west. That way if anything happens we'll be close enough to duck in and make repairs." Tomás runs his finger over the empty, blue space between Key West and the north coast of Cuba. "Then we'll cross the Florida Straights, ninety miles of open water. If the engine holds together it should take fifteen hours each way." Tomás narrows his eyes and looks at me as if he's measuring me. "Nothing but that old engine, this leaky boat, and this," he says, pointing at his forehead, "between us and the deep blue sea, *comprende*?"

I nod.

"Good. We make the jump tomorrow morning before the sun comes up—no turning back," Tomás says as he looks for signs of doubt or fear in my face. He wants to be sure he can count on me. I'm excited and afraid at the same time and I'm not sure which one he'll see on my face, so I turn away.

"No turning back," I say as I step out of the cabin.

"Good," he says and points me toward the cabin. "Now go below and get some rest. I don't want you falling asleep at the wheel."

THE PIRATE'S CHANNEL

When I open my eyes the cabin is hazy; blue smoke is pouring in. I cough and then stumble up to the empty deck. The moon is still out but to the east delicate pink clouds are promising a beautiful sunrise. Tomás is bending into a cloud of exhaust billowing out of the idling engine.

"Did you stay up all night?" I yawn.

"*Sí*, I wanted to put in all the new parts," he says, then shakes his head. "It's too bad that Pops didn't have a carburetor. This one is over the hill." Then he opens a rusty folding chair, sets it up next to the engine, and pats the seat. "It's going to take a lot of tinkering and adjusting to keep this old man running," Tomás says. "Now we'll see how much your friend Bebo taught you about engines."

As I reach around the carburetor I pull a dime from my pocket and adjust the hidden screw. Now the engine is idling a little smoother and not smoking as much, but if I had just the right paper clip I could make it run smoother.

"Good job," Tomás says and then gently pushes the throttle forward, steering south of Key West into the open ocean.

~~~

The sun has just cleared the horizon, when the engine coughs once and then dies. I jiggle the wires to see if one is loose, then I tap the carburetor with my screwdriver and surprise, the engine starts.

For the rest of the morning I sit by the engine like a desperate doctor caring for a patient with a mysterious illness. I use anything I can find in the toolbox and around the boat to keep the old engine running. The nice white tape from the first-aid kit wraps around a leaky hose; the spring from a ballpoint pen keeps the throttle open. I bend the metal ink cartridge and it works almost as well as a paper clip—when it isn't slipping off. I use a coffee can, which I cut open, to cover a hole in the rusty exhaust pipe, and chewing gum to plug up a crack in the distributor. Tomás is amazed. "I would never have thought of that!" He laughs.

In between emergencies I keep busy checking and then tightening the nuts and bolts that the engine shook loose. By the end of the day, the engine is running smoother than ever, so I sit down in my folding chair to rest and watch the sun set.

"Did Bebo teach you all those tricks?" Tomás asks.

"Some," I say, "but most of them I had to make up myself." He did teach me a lot of tricks but the most important thing he taught me was how to think for myself, how to invent.

"Now it's my turn to teach you a thing or two," Tomás says as I follow him to the compass.

Bebo taught me how to find north, south, east, west, and what the points in between were called. He didn't have time to explain how to find your bearings, and then how to keep the boat on the right heading, but Tomás is as good an explainer as Bebo; everything he says makes sense to me.

When he finishes, Tomás takes off his blue captain's cap. "She's all yours, Captain," he says and slaps the cap down on my head. "Keep your eyes on the water, and the lights off. We don't want the Coast Guard to spot us. Now, it's my turn to get some rest."

Gripping the wheel with both hands, I check the compass and then listen to the engine purr. I might have to stand up on my tiptoes to see over the deck, but on this watch I am wearing the cap. I am the captain.

As I watch the dark sea roll by I realize that I never used the important things that Bebo taught me. Before my brothers left me alone I was just like a balloon on a string tagging along behind them. I let them decide, solve, and think for me. Out here, in the dark, if I listen past the drone of the engine, I can feel the big silence rushing by and I can hear myself think. Maybe my brothers were making too much noise for me to hear my own thoughts?

When the moon peeks out from behind the clouds, threads of sparkling gems shimmer on the wake of the boat. I lean over the side to get a closer look.

Suddenly a rubbery black wall rises out of the sea close enough to touch. I jump back as a peaceful eye, the size of a garbage can lid, slides by. It is staring at me as it dips under the waves. Then I hear the sound of rushing water and bells. I look up just in time to see the bow of a freighter bearing down on us.

"Big ship!" I yell and turn the wheel as hard as I can to the right. Tomás runs up as the rusty hull churns by.

"I told you to keep your eye on the water," he says as he inspects the stern of the freighter.

"I did," I gasp. "I saw a whale, and it was looking right at me! Sorry, Tomás, I got distracted, it won't happen again, I promise," I say, as I take the cap off and hand it back to him.

"It's my fault. I should have warned you. This is a shipping channel and, even if they were looking, they can't see us with our lights off," Tomás says and then points at barely visible lights twinkling low on the horizon. "Look, I think that's Havana! Two more hours and we'll be there!"

As we get closer, the lights separate into a cluster of city lights and then a single bright one to the left.

"That is Havana," I say. "The light to the left is El Morro."

Tomás checks his watch. "It took us longer to get here than I thought it would. All the fishing boats are back in the harbor already. If we go in now the light will pick us up and they'll send a boat out to check us out. "

"We can wait out here," I suggest.

Tomás shakes his head. "It's too deep to anchor here, and if I shut down the engine we'll drift too far. "

"I know how we can get into the harbor without the light picking us up! There's a channel right next to the cliffs that will take us under the light. My father told me that pirates and smugglers used it all the time to avoid the light and sneak into the harbor."

"Are you sure?" Tomás asks.

"Yes. We used that channel when we left the harbor to go fishing."

"All right then," Tomás says as he steps aside. "This is your home port. Take us in."

Keeping the boat outside the reach of El Morro's roving beam, I head for the beach to the left of the harbor. Then with the engine idling, I glide into the dark channel between the slick black rocks and stonework of the old Spanish fort.

"Go slow," Tomás whispers. "I can't see a thing."

In the shadow of the light I can't see the cliff, either, but I can feel it. Just like Bebo taught me, I steer by the sound of the engine bouncing off the black walls.

When we slide out of the channel and into the harbor,

Tomás slaps me on the back and puts his captain's hat back on my head. "It's yours. You've earned it. Now, find us a place to anchor near the *Reglas* ferry."

"No problem," I say and steer toward the fishing boats moored by the ferry dock on the east side of the harbor. As Tomás carefully slips the anchor into the water, I cut the engine and nudge into a cluster of boats.

"Let's go below and wait," he whispers.

JUMP

The sunrise is just starting to paint the tops of the buildings pink and gold when the ferry starts up her engines. We have been awake all night. When we heard the fishermen rowing out to their boats we went up on deck and started getting ready. Tomás is looking toward the dock using a plastic toy telescope he found in the trash.

Just as the ferry heads across the bay, he calls out, "There they are! Look," and hands me the telescope.

I scan the crowd on the dock across the bay. "I can't tell who is who. They all look like they're waiting for the ferry."

"Right, this is the only way I could think of to get fourteen people and their luggage on the dock at the same time without the police getting suspicious."

"Yeah, but what will the ferry captain say when they don't get on?" I ask.

"The ferry captain is on a tight schedule. He won't have time to get too curious. We'll swing by right after the ferry leaves."

As the ferry glides into the dock a group of men, women, and children, each carrying a small suitcase, starts walking slowly down the long wooden ramp.

"Fourteen—they're all there," I say and hand the telescope to Tomás but he waves it away.

"Start her up!" he yells.

The engine coughs and wheezes, but it will not start. I grab the screwdriver, fearing that last night's long trip might have been the old engine's last effort. I try tapping the carburetor with the screwdriver, but that doesn't work. Then I jiggle a couple of wires and the engine and finally starts up.

"Give me everything she's got!" Tomás yells.

As we chug across the harbor, Tomás waves at the captain of the ferry on his return trip, then cuts the wheel. My heart is thumping as we jump over the wake of the ferry.

"This is it!" Tomás yells and draws a sharp curve toward the fast-approaching dock. When he gives me the signal I slow the engine to an idle, and then run up to the bow. We slam into the rubber bumpers and Tomás yells, "Secure the bowline!"

I'm about to jump off when I see a man on the dock

wearing a white guayabera—he must be with our group, so I throw him the rope. The rope hits him in the chest. He grabs it as it falls.

Tomás is counting heads as he helps the women and children step into the boat.

I turn away when I hear the man on the dock say, "I— I can't hold this. . . ."

"Just hold it until we're ready to go, then you can jump on; we won't leave you behind," I call to the man. He's holding the rope like he's posing for a picture.

Tomás helps the last couple aboard, then shakes the man's hand.

"I'm proud of you, son!" His mother gathers them all in her arms and they spin slow, like they're dancing to the thump of the idling engine. I can imagine how good that feels.

Then Tomás peels himself off. "We'll catch up later," he says. "Papa, get everyone into the cabin. Julian, we're ready. Release the bowline!"

"Quick! Throw me the line; get on board!" I yell to the man on deck but he's not moving. "Hey, let go!" I yell and pull on the line, but the man pulls back.

"Julian, who is that guy?" Tomás asks.

"Isn't he with us?"

"No, we've got all our people," he answers, and then he says to the man in the white guayabera, "*Hombre*, let go of the rope, now!" But the man will not let go.

"Let go of the rope, please?" I ask nicely.

"I can't!" the man yells. "I know what you're doing. If someone sees me they'll think I was helping you escape."

"Come with us then!"

"Julian! Get back to the throttle!" Tomás orders. "We're ready to go! If he wants to hang on, that's up to him!"

"Why don't you come with us—there is room!" I say to the man.

"How could I?" he cries, as he hops from one foot to the other. "My family! I don't even have my toothbrush!" I can tell that he wants to come. "I wish I hadn't missed my ferry."

"Come with us. You might not get another chance." I feel sorry for him, he probably got up today—just like every day—thinking about his morning coffee, or maybe his job. He was definitely not thinking about leaving on a boat with a bunch of strangers.

"Julian! Someone's coming, get the throttle!" Tomás yells again.

I run back to the engine compartment, leaving the man holding the line.

"Don't worry about him! He'll either let go or end up in the water. Crank it up! We've got to get out of here!"

Tomás steers away from the dock but then the boat stops. I give it a little more gas, the engine strains, coughs once, and dies. I run back to the bow and find the man in the guayabera standing next to the big steel cleat and our line is now tied to it.

Tomás connects the ignition wires again and the engine groans.

"Julian, someone's coming!" Tomás yells. A man dressed in a tan uniform is walking down the ramp. He says something to the guy in the white guayabera, and bends over to untie the boat.

When he stands up I yell, "Bebo!"

"*Hola*, Julian. Didn't expect to see me here, did you?" Bebo smiles. Then he says calmly, "You don't want to make too much noise, somebody might be watching."

"It's good to see you, Bebo," I say, as Tomás runs up behind me.

"Bebo, I've heard a lot about you. I'm Tomás," Tomás says looking around nervously.

"*Mucho gusto, amigo,*" Bebo says and nods toward Tomás. Then he turns to me and smiles. "Good news, Julian, your mother left for Miami a week ago. I'd love to catch up with you but you better get out of here before someone sees you." Bebo reaches into his shirt pocket and pulls out his special paper clip. "Here. From the sound of that engine you're going to need this."

I hold the paper clip as if it's made of gold. "Thanks, Bebo."

"Don't mention it. You better go get that engine started. If they catch you here we'll all go to jail." Then Bebo turns around and starts walking up the ramp.

"Bebo, do you want to come with us?" I call after him.

Bebo turns around and smiles. "Chico, I told you already: they're cooking the omelet just the way I like it."

"Julian! We've got to get out of here!" I hear Tomás say from the wheel.

When I turn back, Bebo's already gone.

As I fit the paper clip into the barrel of the carburetor, I feel an emptiness in my heart. I pry the butterfly open so the right amount of air mixes with the gasoline vapors. That feeling in my heart has been there all this time. The engine sputters, coughs, and starts up. I guess it's like gasoline: it just sits there until you mix it with air and then it burns.

"Thanks, Bebo!" I call out.

Up on the dock the man in the white guayabera has picked up the rope again and he's doing his little shuffling dance, trying to decide if he should stay or go. A few of our passengers have come up on deck. They're talking to him, calling out reasons why he should come with us as Tomás steers the boat away from the dock.

Suddenly the man throws the rope down as if it's a poisonous snake, then runs across the dock. He doesn't stop at the edge. He jumps, his arms and legs spinning in slow motion, like he's swimming in air. He has just made the biggest decision of his life and he's definitely not thinking about landing.

HEROES

Ten miles south of Key West the old engine thumps its last. Even Tomás's father can't get it started. We are drifting out to sea but we aren't about to give up.

Tomás and his father are pulling up pieces of the deck to make a mast and boom. Two of the women and I are collecting shirts and skirts to button and sew together with copper wire to make a sail, when we see the Coast Guard cutter.

As the Coast Guard tows us in, everyone on the boat is laughing and crying. One by one, the men and the women come over to hug Tomás and me, promising to one day repay our kindness. One woman says that she is going to name her first son Julian-Tomás so that no one will ever forget what we've done.

It's late by the time we get to the Coast Guard station in Miami. I am standing at the railing of the gray Coast Guard cutter, looking down at the dock crowded with policemen and firemen, when Tomás walks up to join me. He nods at a newscaster pointing a microphone at a large man gesturing theatrically toward our sinking boat.

"Do you see who that is?" Tomás asked.

"That's Armando! What's he doing here?"

"I hate to admit it, but I think he probably saved our lives," Tomás says.

"What do you mean?"

"The captain of the cutter told me that they got a call to go out and look for us. Armando was the only person who knew about our trip. Knowing Armando, he called the T.V. station and gave them the story to make himself look good, hoping that they'd give him a job as a newsman. He knows that when a T.V. station gets a tip like that, they always call the police, and then the police call the Coast Guard."

A small crowd has gathered around Armando; flash-bulbs pop as he answers questions and poses for the cameras.

Tomás shakes his head and laughs. "Look at him strutting around the dock like the hero."

"He looks like a big rooster to me," I say.

"That big rooster probably saved our lives," Tomás says and puts his hand on my shoulder. "But, if it wasn't for your gold bird and your help with the engine, I could never have made the trip. The best part of it is that you did it because it was the right thing to do." Then he nods at Armando. "He did it for a different reason. It's funny how things worked out."

When they finally let us walk down the ramp, Ramirez is waiting for me on the dock.

"First a runaway, now a hero," he says, then grabs my wrist and leads me to the car. "No detours today, right?"

"No detours; I just want to go home, and I'm not a hero."

"Tell that to the fifteen people back there on the dock," Ramirez says and then locks the door.

On the way back to the camp, we drove through the same neighborhood we passed on the first day. The houses, trees, the red tricycle, even the wooden sign at the gate were all the same. Everything out there had stayed the same, but I knew that I had changed.

When we got to the camp, the car door opened and a pair of beefy, red hands reached in and pulled me out. I grabbed on to the door handle thinking that it might be Caballo, but the smell of mashed potatoes and the stained apron put me at ease.

Dolores pushed me into the kitchen. "This is your lucky day," she said as she slid a plate of steaming meat loaf under my nose. When I told her that I missed her meat loaf, she puffed up proud. "It is good—good enough for the president and the first astronaut," she said with a mysterious smile on her face.

"Did the president remember? Did he call?"

She put her finger to her lips. "Shh, it's all hush-hush—top secret."

Dolores sat down next to me and, as I stuffed chunks of meat loaf into my mouth, she told me about how our "little revolution" turned out. She said that Marta and Angelita had called every number on their list. At first, nothing happened, but they didn't give up. They made another list, collected more dimes, and kept calling until they finally found someone who could help. Dolores laughed and slapped the table. "Things started to change around here real quick after that! Before Ol' Caballo knew what hit him, he was on his way to that orphanage in Denver."

"Isn't that where my brothers are?" I asked. It would be a sad day for them to have Caballo follow them there.

"That's where they were," she said. "I heard they left last week and went to live with your uncle up in Connecticut. I'm sure the police told you that your mother's there, too." Then Dolores dug into her apron pocket and handed me three letters. "Here—letters from your brothers. They came in while you were away."

"Thank you, Dolores!" I said as I leafed through the letters.

"Don't thank me; Angelita collected them and then gave them to me before she left to go live with her brother." Then Dolores looked up at the clock and said, "Now, if I were you, I'd go see if I could find my old friends, before I hang an apron on you. I got to get dinner ready."

As I stepped out into the dusty yard Ramirez was just getting into his car.

"Hey, *Cubanito*," he yelled as the car started to drive off. "Stop," I heard him say to the driver. "What's the hurry? I want to say good-bye to my friend."

I ran up to the car, and we shook hands. "Julian, thanks for letting me catch you," he laughed and then took his sunglasses off. "Cases like yours are what make my job worthwhile; I just wish they all worked out as well," he said, and the car started moving again. "I guess it's good-bye for now. Maybe I'll see you in Havana next year!" he called out the window.

I waved good-bye thinking about Lucia, the girl who sold hats and made drawings for the tourists. I wonder if she ever saved up enough money for her mother's plane ticket?

Besides Dolores, Ramirez was the only familiar face I found in the camp. The dormitory, dusty baseball field, and the pool were crowded with new kids. Where did they find all these new kids and what did they do with the old ones?

A group of girls are sitting around the picnic table weaving fancy palm hats with swans swimming on top. I walk over hoping that Marta will be there. I ask who taught them how to make the hats, and they said that it was a girl named Raquel who had left a week ago. Marta probably taught Raquel and then she taught these girls.

I sat on the shed roof reading my brothers' letters. The

first letter was about snowfalls that buried the windows and doors, and trapping them inside with nuns that smelled like mothballs. The second one told about the tricks they had to learn and the things they had to do just to avoid getting into fights. Alquilino described it best: "It is very important to avoid fights as the inmates here are big and dangerous."

The last letter announced that Caballo had got beaten up on the first day there. "Now he follows us everywhere we go," Gordo wrote. "This morning I woke up and there was Caballo sitting next to our bunks with that weird smile on his face. Now he wants to be our friend. Yesterday he returned your dumb drawing book!"

I had barely finished the last letter when I heard someone calling my name, telling me to get ready. It was the new director.

"I haven't even unpacked!" I answered.

"If you don't mind flying alone to Connecticut, you can leave today."

"Of course not; I've flown before," I said as if I had done it a thousand times.

I am feeling very grown up when I board the airplane all alone, carrying my blue suitcase—I'm not scared at all.

When we land in Connecticut, I find a man holding up a cardboard sign with my name on it. I introduce myself to him.

"Welcome to Connecticut. I'm Mr. Mooney," he says,

and then tries to grab my suitcase. When I won't let go, he says, "Independent little guy, aren't you?"

As he drives out of the airport, Mr. Mooney keeps telling me how lucky I am that my uncle was willing to take our whole family, even though he has four kids of his own. "Some kids are not as lucky, you know!"

"I know," I say, thinking about Lucia and all the other kids that disappeared from the camp. I hope they are all back together with their families.

"You're going to live in a brand-new neighborhood," Mr. Mooney says as we turn onto a freshly paved road. At the bottom of the hill there are gray foundations rising out of the mud. Near the top, the framed houses without shingles or siding look just like birdcages made of yellow sticks. On the other side of the hill the houses are all finished. All the houses are the same. They all have a green patch of lawn in front, but each one is painted a different color. Why would they build the same house over and over again?

"This is it," Mr. Mooney announces. My stomach starts to jump as he slows down.

CONNECT-Y-CUT

The woman standing in the middle of my uncle's living room holding a vacuum cleaner looks a lot like my mother, but I'm not sure. I've never seen my mother near a vacuum cleaner. Maybe that's why I can't recognize her, or maybe I just got too good at forgetting.

"Julian!" the woman yells, drops the vacuum cleaner, and then throws her arms around me. I bury my head in the soft place at the base of her neck. My mother's warmth and the waves of perfumed hair crumble the sandcastle walls I had built around her memory. Now I'm home and swimming in her warm sea again, barely aware that my brothers are standing in the doorway. They come closer to poke and measure me, and then grudgingly declare that I did grow a little. But they're just looking at my skin—the outside of me.

Safe with my mother and brothers around me, I feel like I've been holding my breath for a long time and now I can finally exhale. But I can still feel something hard and brittle around my heart. I think that's the shell I had to grow to be able to make it through all that time I was alone. I think it's going to take a long time to melt that shell.

When my younger cousins come thumping and tumbling down the stairs, they jump around Alquilino and Gordo, begging to be picked up and spun around.

My brothers have grown, too. Alquilino has more little black wires growing out of his chin and Gordo has an angry red scar on his forearm. I'm sure they have a lot of stories to tell. As they bounce and toss the cousins between them, I wonder if my brothers have that little hard place inside of them, too.

My mother is smiling. She doesn't seem to hear the high, anxious note the vacuum cleaner is now singing as it tries to swallow my aunt's new drapes.

"Where's Papi?" I ask, and her smile tightens.

"They didn't let him out."

"Why?"

"He's building a hospital and they won't let him leave until he finishes."

"When is he coming?"

"I don't know, Julian, but we're all trying to get him out

as fast as possible. Now come see your room," she says and leads me downstairs.

The large bed in the too-small room leaves barely enough space to squeeze around it. I'm picturing myself stretching out alone in the big bed when she says, "You'll sleep here with your brothers. There is plenty of room for all of you. Now, let's open up your suitcase."

"Don't you want to know where I went? Aren't you curious about what I did?" I say, hoping I can at least get a chance to explain before she finds out.

"Of course, Julian. But first . . ." she points at the bed.

I swallow hard, swing the suitcase up on the bed and then open it. She picks up the cracked plate sitting on top of a tangled knot of damp clothes. As her fingers worry the rough edges of the hole in the middle where the fish should be, a tear crawls down her cheek. "You gave this to Papi for Father's Day, remember?"

"I was missing one piece, but I glued it back together the best I could; I thought you'd be happy to have it," I say, and wipe the tear away.

"Thank you, Julian. When we get our own house, I'll hang it where everyone can see it, so we don't forget," she says as she stares past the knot of my wet clothes. "What a mess!" she says and then runs her fingers along the inside of the suitcase. I'm starting to get nervous because I know what's coming.

"I had to jump into the river from a bridge; that's why

my clothes are all wet," I blurt out. "It was higher than the high diving board at the beach and then I went on a boat. . . ."

Her hand stops near the corner. "You can tell me all about it later, Julian." She's found the empty compartment.

"Where is it?" she says in a hoarse whisper.

"I traded it for . . ." The words mumble out.

"Julian, I trusted you to take care of it. Where is it?"

Alquilino and Gordo are hovering over me, shaking their heads. As soon as they came in, they squeezed all the air out of the too-small room. I'm having a hard time catching my breath.

"Tomás, he needed the money," I gasp. "He took me in, fixed up an old boat; there were fourteen people on a dock in Havana and he couldn't let them down!" I try to get it all out but still, she's not listening.

"I was going to sell it and use the money to get Papi out," she says and sinks down onto the bed. "Now we have nothing." Suddenly the room has gotten even smaller.

"My friend Tomás promised he would get it back."

"He promised?" my mother asks as if I was crazy to give it away on a promise.

She hides her face in her hands. "We have nothing, *nada*!" she cries. All the air and the confidence that had bloomed around my heart starts to leak and wither, but the hard shell is still there, still insisting.

"Tomás risked his life on a leaky boat to go back," I say.

"He kept his word to them and he'll keep his word to me!" I yell.

Alquilino sits down and puts his arm around Mami. Gordo leans against the wall and shakes his head. I don't know what else to say. The room is quiet except for the echo of my words, buzzing like angry bees in my ear.

"You should let him explain," Alquilino says softly.

My mother gets up. "You don't understand," she says and scoops up my clothes and bumps past Alquilino.

She stops in the doorway and asks, "Well, did they get out?"

"Yes, six men, five women, and four children."

My mother stays up washing my clothes so I'll have something to wear for my first day of school. I stay up late, too, listening to her mumbling and ironing late into the night.

If she had seen their grateful faces, heard the nice things they said, she would understand why I did it.

In the morning I wake up to find my mother folding my clean clothes at the foot of the bed. She sets aside my dress pants and shirt. "I want you to look good for your first day at school, make friends."

I have never set foot in an American school so I have no way of knowing for sure, but I have a feeling that the clothes she set out are not going to help me fit in.

My mother insists that Alquilino and Gordo walk me to the bus stop even though it's at the bottom of the hill and you can see it from the kitchen window.

"I'm old enough to walk by myself," I say.

"A boy your age should not be walking alone."

I could tell her that I rode buses all over Miami by myself, jumped from a bridge into a river, sold lemonade on a street where everyone was a stranger, but I don't think this is the right time. That will have to wait.

As the yellow bus chugs up the hill, Gordo turns to me with a smirk on his face. "Julian, don't be afraid. If anybody bothers you just let me know," he says.

"I'm *not* afraid!" I snap back.

"Little Julian sure looks scared to me," he says in his old singsong, insulting way.

"I'm just worried about the bird, that's all."

"You should be worried. You really stuck your foot in it this time," Gordo says as the bus doors creak open. "Mami should have known better than to trust you with it!"

"You don't know what you're talking about, Gordo!" I shout and climb into the bus.

I stomp past the driver and I'm halfway down the aisle when I notice that everybody is staring at me like I'm from outer space. The last seat is empty, so I drop my eyes and follow the rubber floor mat to the last row.

Gordo is standing right outside my window. I open it, thinking that he wants to apologize. "What do you want?" I ask.

Gordo jams his thumb into his chest. "Remember, if anybody gives you any trouble," he yells so that everybody on the bus can hear him, "just let me know. I'll take care of them for you."

Great, now everybody is going to think that I need my brothers to take care of me. "I can take care of myself," I say and snap the window shut.

The schoolyard is brimming with kids running across the wet grass, or huddled in bunches around the swings. As I wait for the bus to empty, I see a circle of kids forming by our bus door. I'll be the last one off so they must be waiting for me. How could they know I was coming?

There is nowhere else to go so I step into the circle. The kids standing around me are wearing jeans, khakis, T-shirts, and sweatshirts. I'm dressed in a green silk shirt, gold linen pants, and two-toned shoes. I was hoping that I could blend in, just disappear into the crowd, but now I know there's no chance of that. They're all looking at me like I'm the parakeet in a flock of sparrows.

A stocky boy walks across the empty space toward me. "Hello," I say, but he keeps coming until he's standing so close that I can count the freckles on his face. We look at each other; I try to smile but he's giving me the look. It's the same look in English as it is in Spanish. I should have known that they'd have bullies here, too. He bumps his chest into mine and right away I know what he wants. I can't fight in my silk shirt—my mother would kill me! It's my first day of school and I'm supposed to be making friends, not enemies. I lower my head and try to walk past him, but he steps in front of me. He pushes me against the bus and I feel the anger bubbling up inside me. I push back hard, hard enough to topple a Caballo-sized bully. I follow the boy as he flies backward, trips, and lands on his back. I jump on top of him, pinning his arms down with my knees. The crowd is yelling; the boy is squirming beneath me. I raise my fist but I notice his freckles are melting into his angry red face, and there is a spark of fear in his eyes. Suddenly, I understand what Angelita was trying to tell me about bullies. They wear the same look, because they're all trying to hide the same fear. They're afraid that if they don't push and bully, someone will push and bully them. They have to be that way. That thought suddenly sucks all the anger right out of me.

Now I don't feel like fighting, but I'm still sitting on his chest and the crowd is yelling, rooting for the boy to squash the newcomer-parakeet. How can they be angry with me? They don't even know me.

I stand up and the crowd closes in. They're shouting insults at the boy because he's letting me get away. I feel bad for him so I reach down to help him up, but he grabs the sleeve of my green silk shirt instead of my hand. Just then somebody pulls on my right ear, jerks my head around, and I hear a tearing sound.

A gray-haired teacher is wagging her finger at me; my ripped sleeve is lying on the boy's chest like a deflated snake. I twist and wiggle as far away from her as I can, without her yanking my ear off, and make a stab for the sleeve. The teacher pulls me back. I yell, *"¡Caramba!"* Then she lets go and I grab my sleeve.

"I am Mrs. Johnson." The teacher introduces herself. Then she launches into a lecture about fighting. "Are you listening to me?" she asks. I can understand what she's saying but I don't answer. I'm trying to slip my arm back into the empty sleeve.

Then she shakes me. "Can you hear me?" she asks as I just stare up at her strange, metal gray eyes.

"Do you understand me?" she asks, and looks at me as if I'm a two-legged riddle, a problem that she has to solve. Without waiting for an answer she hurries me through the crowded hallways.

"After we get you settled, I'll send you down to get your hearing tested," she says loud enough for everyone to hear. She leads me into her classroom and then props me up in front of the class.

"This is *Julie-Ann*," she says—I wince when she mispronounces my name. "He's from the tropical island of Cuba."

I try to correct her. "My name is *Who-li-an*," I say, but it's too late.

"Julie-Ann is from a tropical island," I hear a boy snicker.

Mrs. Johnson pulls down a map of North America that covers the blackboard and points at "my tropical island." On this map it looks like a short hop from the tip of Florida to Havana—a lot shorter than I remember it.

"Do you have any questions for your new classmates?" Mrs. Johnson asks.

A girl with fire-red hair raises her hand, but Mrs. Johnson ignores her, pointing at a sleepy-looking kid in the back of the room instead.

"Oscar?"

"Did you live in a tree house like Tarzan?" he asks, and the class laughs.

"Did you have a T.V.?" "Where did they put the antenna?" "Did you eat off plates?" The questions tumble out of the laughing class, each one sillier than the last, and I stare at my two-toned shoes.

The red-haired girl still has her hand up but now she is waving it back and forth like she's washing a big window.

"Yes, Darlene, do you have a question?" Mrs. Johnson asks and then warns, "Just one, Darlene."

"My mother read in the paper that parents were sending their children out of your country all alone. Is that how you came?" Darlene asks and calmly arranges her braids. "My mother said that she would never, ever send me away like that—all alone to a strange place, even if it was the United States of America. I mean, why didn't they just buy a ticket and leave with you? Didn't you miss them and who took care of you?"

If I could talk, I would tell her that I had asked myself the same question over and over again. Then I would tell the class that we have houses, cars, and televisions just like they do here and that we watched Tarzan movies in a brand-new theater that had the coldest air-conditioning in all of Havana. I would even love to tell them about the camp, Caballo, and the trip on Tomás's boat, but I feel naked standing up here with just one sleeve and I'm afraid if I open my mouth the words won't line up, and then they'll really laugh at me.

"I mean how bad could it be that they would . . ." the girl continues.

"Darlene!" Mrs. Johnson shouts. "I said one question!"

Then Mrs. Johnson takes me to my seat in the back of the room. I open the desk and stick my head inside as if I'm looking for something. It smells like old milk in here, but it feels good to be out of sight, even if it is just for a second.

I try to follow what Mrs. Johnson is saying, but the words I don't understand start to pile up.

From the last seat of the last row all I can see is the back of everyone's heads. It looks like they're walking away from me, moving ahead, but I'm stuck behind a pile of words that I can't climb over. I'm getting left behind, and I can't tell them to stop. I don't belong here and I guess it doesn't matter.

I never felt this way when I was on Tomás's boat. There, I made a difference—he told me so. It mattered that I was there.

I rummage through the desk and find a stack of white paper and colored pencils. I'm never lost when I draw, so I start a picture of our house with a television antenna on the roof—our car in the driveway. The next one is of the man with the beard, pointing his cigar—dictating; then a golden swallow with ruby wings flying over Tomás in his boat with fifteen grateful people waving and smiling on deck. I draw one picture after the other until I run out of paper. When I look up, Mrs. Johnson is busy writing math problems on the blackboard. I follow along for a little while, happy to see that math is the same in English as it is in Spanish, but it doesn't take long to get bored; we did the same problems last year.

I gaze out the window at the strange red trees and discover that they are not always red—they're turning red. The trees in Cuba would never turn red for no reason at all. I could ask Mrs. Johnson why, but I think she's forgotten about me. She hasn't called on me or come back here all day. Maybe I've become invisible. Maybe that's good because then she won't notice if I drift off into a daydream.

It's easy to turn the red leaves into a blue sea and then to imagine a fishing boat bobbing on the waves. My father, Bebo, and my brothers are all standing around the fighting chair as I work the rod. I can hear the reel singing, my brothers cheering me on. My arms are tired but I'm not letting go. I am about to land the biggest marlin we've ever hooked, when I hear a bell ringing off in the distance. A gray calico pattern appears like a transparent screen between the fish and me. When the pattern shifts, the boat, the blue sea, and my brothers all disappear, and Mrs. Johnson is standing over me in her gray calico dress. The class is up and gathering their books, chattering away as they file out of the room. Mrs. Johnson is holding my drawing of Dolores with her meat loaf and the tin-can spaceship in orbit behind her.

"Hoo-lian! These drawings—they tell your story?" she asks, then she points at Dolores. "And who is this?"

"Dolores," I say and sit up.

"Would you tell me about Dolores?" Mrs. Johnson asks.

I stare into her eyes. Now they're sparkly blue with curiosity.

"You want me to tell?" I ask, surprised to see she's interested. She's the very first person to ask. No one in my own family has asked; they say they're too busy, but I have a feeling that they're just not interested. After all, how interesting could the story be if it happened to me?

Mrs. Johnson sits down on the windowsill next to me. I start by telling her about Dolores, how she met President Kennedy, and her delicious, soon-to-be-orbiting meat loaf.

"Julian, your classmates would love to hear that story, especially since tomorrow is the day they're planning to launch an astronaut into orbit! Tomorrow morning I'll put your drawings up on the board, and you can start telling us about Cuba and how you got here. The children will love hearing about your great adventure." Then Mrs. Johnson smiles and says, "Julian, we are glad that you're here."

As I walk across the schoolyard I spot the boy who

ripped my shirt standing in front of the door of my bus. His friends, standing by the swings, are watching me as I slow down to try to think of something I can say or do to get on that bus without fighting. Then Darlene, the girl with the red braids, runs up and starts walking next to me.

"Watch," she says as we get near the bus. Darlene gets right in the boy's face and snarls, "You have to move." She's one head bigger than him and by the tone of her voice I can tell she's not going to back away. I think the boy knows that, too.

"This has nothing to do with you, Darlene," the boy warns as he shifts nervously from one foot to the other.

"This has nothing to do with him, either," Darlene snaps back. "You don't even know him well enough to like or dislike him!"

When the boy hesitates, I step forward and thrust my hand out. First he looks back at his friends, and then at me, and—surprise—he shakes my hand.

"I'm Julian."

"I know, I know," he says, as I pump his hand.

"I'm Chuck," he mumbles, pulls his hand back, and then walks away.

"You're home free for today!" Darlene says and pushes me into the bus. "Get in there before his big brother shows up."

"Big brother?"

Darlene laughs. "Don't worry, I'll show you how to get

around him tomorrow." She flashes me a sly smile, and says, "Julian, you're not alone here."

On the way home I'm thinking about Mrs. Johnson's blue eyes, Darlene's sly smile, and what she said. I'm not too worried about meeting his older brother. He couldn't be worse than Caballo.

At the bus stop Gordo takes one look at my sleeveless shirt and dirty pants and laughs. "Looks like you lost," he says. "What's his name?"

"I didn't lose and I can take care of myself."

When I get home my mother is sitting at the kitchen table with a small cardboard box in front of her on the table. She hands me the box and doesn't ask about my clothes.

"This came special delivery for you," she says.

I recognize the neatly printed address immediately. "It's from Tomás!"

I carefully pull off the tape, then lift out a folded Pirate Angel place mat. The golden swallow with ruby wings is sleeping peacefully on a bed of shredded newspaper.

"It's here!" I yell and wave it around for all to see, and then I hand it to my mother. The instant her finger touches it, the icy, bitter expression on her face starts to melt, and I can almost see the old sweetness in her eyes.

"Julian, I'm sorry I doubted you. It's been so hard, first to lose you and your brothers, and now your father." My mother lowers her head.

When I hug her, I hear something rising from deep

down in her chest. Her sobs sound like little waves breaking and then breathing back to sea.

We all crowd around the small kitchen table to hear my mother read the letter from Tomás. The two families listen quietly as my mother reads about the stolen compass, the trip in a leaky boat with a fickle old engine, and how we snuck into Havana Harbor. When she gets to the part about how I kept the old engine going with tape and a paper clip, Gordo and Alquilino both raise their eyebrows and look at me as if she's talking about a different Julian.

"Without Julian and that little bird, fifteen people would not have been reunited with their families. You will always be welcome in my home. Someday and over dinner and a cold glass of Tomás-ade, I would love to hear about your trip."

When she finishes, she puts down the letter and starts clapping slowly. My aunt Marta and my uncle José stand up, then my little cousins join in. When Alquilino and Gordo finally get up, they clap a couple times like their arms were really tired and then sit back down. My mother puts her arms around me. "Julian, you did the right thing. Tonight you can start telling me the whole story. Tomorrow I'm going to sell this little bird, and we'll have enough money to get Papi out. Then our family will be together again."

We all raise our glasses, cups, and flan dishes, anything we can click together. "To our new home," Aunt Marta says.

"Where anything is possible," my mother adds.

It's a school night but we stay up talking and joking like we used to. By the time we finally get to bed the sad dark cloud that hung over our heads is in tatters. I can feel it blowing away.

For the second day of school I'm dressed like a normal person. I let Alquilino and Gordo walk ahead of me on the way to the bus stop. The little transistor radio they bought is pressed in between their heads. They look like Siamese twins, joined at the ear.

Suddenly, Gordo jerks his head back and yells, "*Apollo* is in orbit!"

Alquilino points at the sky. "The astronaut—he's up there in a tin can!" He's shouting but I can barely hear him. Bulldozers are gobbling up the green pastures on either side of the busy road, turning them into little patches of lawn.

Just then a dump truck growls by, and my brothers disappear into a cloud of dust. There is a whole tree—leaves, roots, and all—in the back of the truck, as if a giant had just yanked it out of the ground. The tips of the roots look like hands waving—waving up at the man in orbit above us. I bet that astronaut is eating Dolores's deluxe meat loaf for lunch. Why not? My mother said that almost anything is possible here. What a place to begin again!